Sylvie the Second

Sylvie
the
Second

KAELI BAKER

submarine

© Kaeli Baker 2015

ISBN 978-0-9941065-3-7

Cover image: Connie McDonald
facebook.com/ConnieMcDonaldPhotography

Cover design: Mākaro Press
Book design and typesetting: Paul Stewart
Editor: Mary McCallum

Printed by Printstop, Wellington, NZ

submarine
Mākaro Press, po box 41 032
Eastbourne New Zealand
www.makaropress.co.nz

To the ones who feel invisible

One

Emergency departments definitely have bad vibes. Fluorescent lights etching worry lines in people's faces. Feet tapping on the linoleum floor. The wails of small children, and the nervous looks of parents who are trying to be calm, but would rather throw their grown-up hats out the window.

Silent crying, stifled sniffles and hands clasped in unity. All the while, waiting, waiting, waiting.

All eyes on the clock. The staff on the desk looking through you. Doctors and nurses walking briskly – *why don't they run?* – and murmuring amongst themselves. Stretchers pushed by paramedics with strings of panicked family members rushing behind. The occasional crash trolley.

The smell of barely concealed fear.

I know this, because I've been to a few in my time.

Not as a patient, but as a family member. Not so much a concerned family member, as a family member too young to be left at home alone.

At 15, I went along because I was curious and because I cared, but mostly because I was scared. I spent the long hours distracting myself from the situation at hand by people-watching, and guessing what people were in for and which doctor was banging which nurse.

I'd been a regular in the emergency department since I was 12. My sister, Cate, was a bit of a frequent flyer since she had a habit of trying to kill herself. On this particular night, she'd overdosed for the kabillionth time. It was me who found her when I snuck into her room to steal her iPod. She was lying on the bed, iPod in ears, and – *crapola!* – a bottle of benzos in hand. Empty. So much for a night stealing her tunes.

I called for Pamela Panic who flew into the room like a Boeing 737, scooped her up, and called out to Dave in a panic-filled pitch to phone an ambulance. I could hear my father's 'damn it all!' downstairs as he tried to locate the cordless phone. This was his usual expletive when Calamity Cate tried to top herself, earning him the nickname Damn-it-all Dave. My nickname for him. I liked using alliteration. It was another thing that kept me occupied during the long hours in ED. Hostile hospitals, dodgy doctors, nasty nurses, pained patients etc.

Pamela Panic was pale and pacing – *take that!* – yes, my mother was perpetually on the precipice of pathetic, wringing her hands and holding her forehead as if she was the one who was dying, not Calamity Cate.

'Sylvie, go and get me some water will you?'

That's me. Sylvie the Second. My parents were always so caught up with my sister, who went quickly from girl wonder to train wreck, that I was introduced as 'This is Sylvie, our second.' Second guess, second choice, second best. My whole life I'd *felt* second best, standing lamely in Cate's gloriously overwhelming shadow. Now that she was sick, I'd been demoted further. I was invisible.

I pressed down on the tap and watched the water tumble from the water cooler into the polystyrene cup. I loved water. As a child I would sit in the bath with Cate, filling up toy buckets and dumping them over her head. She would cry and Pamela Panic would rush in and tell me off for upsetting the first child. The golden child.

Thing is, I didn't do it to upset her. I did it because I loved watching the water splash out of the bucket, and instead of hurting her when it hit her head, it would assimilate to the shape, and run gently down her face and around her ears and make her golden hair look so smooth and more rustic in colour. I loved that water didn't hurt when it hit you.

Unless you hit it first.

Cate jumped off a bridge last year and landed

in the river below. She broke both her legs and had bruising to boot. But although the water hurt her that time, it still saved her life. A couple of guys in a kayak drifted past soon after and noticed her broken form floating peacefully on the river's surface. I thought it was amazing how water could splash playfully over her head, break her legs with its strength, and save her life with its buoyancy. I also believe it's no coincidence that our last name is Rivers.

I carried the cup of water back to my mother, who took it with no comment, but pushed a rogue piece of hair behind my ear. Her eyes hurt to look at. I looked away.

Damn-it-all Dave was *tsking* and getting all huffy about a child crying nearby. He was almost always angry these days. I didn't think I'd ever really existed for my father. He was a career man and didn't have time for the trivial ways of little girls. Cate and I used to agree that it was because he'd always wanted boys.

'Mr and Mrs Rivers?'

The parents bustled over to the doctor. They'd gone through this so many times. The doctor was a freakin' babe for an old guy – he must've been in his mid-30s or something. He had sandy hair that fell across his eyes and lips that looked like they were hiding something. He smiled at me – *at me! He can see me!* – before addressing the olds.

'We've pumped her stomach and stabilised her. Just waiting for bloods to come back, but in the meantime we're shifting her upstairs to the medical ward. You can meet her up there.'

My parents thanked him while I attempted to act like a concerned sister/serene beauty – *cough* – by way of grinning at him stupidly, trying to pretend that it was normal to be standing in a hospital at 2am on a school night with a kamikaze sister. He returned my questionable efforts with another smile, but it was one I'd seen a lot. A sympathy smile. Ugh.

We would've got to the medical ward to see Calamity Cate a whole lot faster if we hadn't got lost. Hospital corridors are like rabbit warrens. One wrong turn and you're in the morgue or something. We'd only moved to Woodbridge about three months ago and had only been to the local hospital one other time. Cate had periods of managing okay, but then something would happen and she'd start wanting to die again.

I trailed behind my parents and watched Dave put his hand on Pamela's shoulder. She shrugged him off as if the weight of his hand was the straw that would break her.

I cleared my throat.

'Any chance someone remembered to record *Modern Family*?'

'What do you think, Sylvie?' My father growled.

'Um. No?'

'No. I didn't even get time to finish the crossword.'

'Oh, David, for the love of God!' said my mother.

'Surely there are more important things. You can watch it online, Sylvie.'

When we finally found the ward, the nurse showed us to her room.

'She's asleep. She'll probably only be in for the night.'

Pamela nodded automatically. How many times had we left Cate in the medical ward overnight for observation? She always looked pretty peaceful when she slept. God knew what went on in that head though. It didn't really bear thinking about, and when I tried I didn't understand it. We were only allowed to stay ten minutes since it was well past visiting hours. Fine by me – I always felt irritated by those beeps and dings that are the soundtrack of the wards.

On the way out, I had to stop and tie my shoelace. When I stood back up, my parents were nowhere in sight. Hurrying around the corner to the exit, I spotted them walking out the door. They were walking side by side but so far apart you could've slotted a suburb in between them.

What hurt me, though, was the fact that they hadn't even noticed I wasn't with them.

Yeah, that hurt.

Like a river breaking my legs.

Two

When my alarm went off I nearly had a cardiac arrest. My eyes felt like someone had poured sand in them and my whole body ached. I threw the covers back. It was 3am by the time I'd crawled into bed and dissolved into sleep, and now it was 6:30am and time for school. Fantastic.

I didn't go to school because I was smart. I didn't go to socialise. I didn't even go because I had to. I could easily have got my mother to write a note – she would've – she couldn't have cared less. I went because going to school was normal.

Rain trickled down my bedroom windows.

Picking up my jeans and a pink and grey T-shirt off the floor, I shuffled down the hall to the shower. The warm water washed off the previous night and relaxed my tired bones. The mirror revealed shadows under my eyes, and my hair, as always, was a tangled mess of mousiness. A lump rose in my throat from nowhere – *what the hell?*

Sad. Ugly. Fat.

God.

Maybe I was due for my period.

I flung open the door and walked down the driveway. By the time I got home from school Calamity Cate would be back in the house.

I dragged my feet to the bus stop.

I didn't get what was happening to my sister. Instead of being sad and worried about Cate, I was mostly just ferociously angry. It made me angry that she'd got herself into this state. It made me angry because I thought she must have been making it up. It made me angry because I didn't know how to help her. And it made me angry because even though she was bonkers, she *still* hogged the spotlight.

At school I took my place at a desk next to Lorelei. We'd known each other since we were children – we'd started school together at the local primary and moved up to the high school at the same time. When my family moved, I'd refused to shift schools. It was something stable in my otherwise bizarre life. The only downside was the longer commute. I shimmied out of my jacket and threw a tired smile in Lorelei's direction. She glanced at me briefly and went back to talking to Samara.

Lorelei was really my only friend I guess, apart

from Bookish Belle in my English class. I hung out with Belle quite a bit, but she was so painfully nerdy it sometimes cramped my style. No one noticed her. Everyone noticed Lorelei.

Lorelei had morphed over the past few months into one of those gross barbies in the 'popular' group – *popular with whom, each other?* – who had dubbed themselves 'Models Inc'. She now wore as much make-up as the school would tolerate, had gone blonde and straightened her hair. I think she *thought* she looked like a playboy bunny or some kind of movie star. What she actually looked like was a child playing dress-ups. She would endlessly flick her stupid hair around the place and talk about how much guys liked blondes.

Boring. Vapid. Ugliness.

'Ohmigod, you should've seen the boys on the bus today,' she was saying to Samara. 'One of them was checking me out and he was the hottest by far, even though they were all hot, and then he asked if we were going to this party next weekend! He's totally going to ask me out!'

Samara looked bored and nodded vaguely, far more interested in texting. Sensing that she was losing her audience but not willing to have her story ignored, Lorelei turned to me instead.

I was busy trying to focus my eyes. My stomach was rumbling.

'You should see this guy,' she continued, unfazed.

'He's got these beautiful green eyes and *muscles!*' she squealed.

I forced myself to look at her, but her stupid made-up face made me want to punch it. I didn't say anything. I didn't know what to say in those situations, not being very well versed on the subject of boys.

Lorelei rolled her eyes and said in a *way* too loud voice,

'God, Sylvie, are you a lesbian or something?!'

I swear the entire class stopped their gossiping, texting and hurriedly-scribbled homework and stared at me awkwardly. I felt my cheeks flush. My heart was thudding. My palms were sweating and I felt so homicidal towards Lorelei at that moment that I had to leave.

Suddenly I wasn't invisible and for the wrong reasons.

I ran out of the class and down the hall and pushed through the heavy double doors. My eyes were burning with sleep-sand *and* tears now and I felt sick. The truth was I didn't know if I was gay, straight, bi, or nothing. Was that okay?

Temporarily vision impaired, I smacked into a body.

'Woah!' said the owner.

I blinked hard and looked up. Oh. Shit. Adam Allegro – *no, not my sad alliteration, that's actually his name!* – was looking down at me with shock which melted quickly into something like … concern?

No way.

'Hey. Are you okay?'

I sniffed, aware that I must have been turning a flattering shade of beetroot.

'I'm fine.' I croaked, disentangled myself and walked away.

Fantastic. He's going to go to class and hear all about how I'm a lesbian. Even if I'm not. All because Lore-liar is exactly that: a liar. The rumours that girl had spread about me in the past ... Could someone please tell me why I called her a friend?

I turned at the bottom of the steps and looked up. He was still watching me. Adam was the most beautiful boy I'd ever seen, and he had seen *me*.

Well shit, I thought.

Maybe I am straight.

Three

My phone rang.

Belle. I wiped away my tears and pressed ignore. No one was home when I'd got back – I'd assumed they must have been picking Calamity up from the hospital. My bedroom had been filled with the sound of my sobs, and when I had no tears left my face felt warm and wet. It didn't make anything better. I just felt pathetic and ugly.

My phone beeped.

Voice message from Belle: 'Hey, are you okay? I heard you ran out of class today and something about a stupid lesbian comment. She's not a very good friend, Sylvie. Call me when you can, I want to make sure you're all good. Um. It's Belle, by the way. But you probably knew that because your phone would've showed ... Anyway. Bye. Ring me. Bye.'

She was good to me. I felt like I should honour that since I knew she would be genuinely worried, but I couldn't face talking. I didn't trust my voice. I punched out a text and hit send.

> Me: Hey, thx 4 checkn up. All G, just tired and pissed off.

The reply came back fast. I knew without looking at the clock that it must be lunchtime. She would never text in class.

> Belle: Okay. Let me know if you need to talk.

Bookish Belle never abbreviated anything. To her it was the ultimate abuse of the English language. I was surprised she tolerated my texts at all, but I was too lazy to spell everything out. She knew what I meant.

Still, no one was home. I checked Facebook before venturing out into the hall, puffy and snotty and unkempt. I'd started to feel uneasy. Cate had posted a status before she'd taken the overdose: 'Better to light a match than burn the house down.' What the hell? I thought it was a vaguely familiar quote, but she'd obviously got it mixed up. Her account seriously needed a moderator.

What if something had gone wrong at the hospital? What if she'd died while I was here feeling sorry for myself? I looked around the house for a note to tell me what was going on. I double-checked my phone. No missed calls or messages from either Pamela or Dave. I decided to ring Pamela's cell.

'Hello?'

'Mum, where are you?'

'Sylvie, Cate's not good – she created mayhem on the ward this morning. She's been seen by the crisis team and is being admitted to the mental health unit again.'

Again. The last time she went in was when she'd broken her legs in the river.

'Nice of you to tell me,' was all I could think to say.

'Well it's not all about you is it, Sylvie?' Pamela of the Panic Pandemonium snapped.

I could feel the bite through the receiver. I hung up on her.

Nothing is ever about me.
I just want to be someone else.
Someone else …

Struck by a sudden brainwave, I grabbed the laptop and logged into my online banking. My cheque account was perpetually empty, but my savings were looking pretty good. The grandparents would always send $100 every birthday and Christmas in a card from Australia, or Tahiti, or America, or wherever their yacht was at that given moment. What a life! I couldn't wait to retire.

Being a bit averse to shopping, I generally just banked my money and let it build up. Now was the time it would come in handy. I transferred a chunk to my cheque account, grabbed my bag and left the house.

First stop was the chemist. I stood and stared at the variety of hair dyes available. I had no idea what would suit me, but I didn't really care. I just wanted to be different; not a Models Inc/Barbie, but not me. I selected a stand-out colour – Bright Cherry Red.

Next stop: *Easy Cosmetics*. Black eyeliner, dark lipstick, mascara and nail polishes. I swiped my Eftpos card so many times I was surprised I didn't get tennis elbow. I raided cheap jewellery stores and op shops and by the time I got home, I had armloads of items, which I dumped on my bed.

Still no one home.

In the bathroom I followed the instructions on the red hair dye. When I got out of the shower after washing it all out, it looked like someone had been killed in there.

As if I care. They probably won't even notice.

I dried my hair off and straightened it with Cate's straighteners, which had previously been confiscated and were kept in my room, away from her. I muddled through the eyeliner and eyeshadow and ran the plum-coloured lipstick over my lips.

Next: an outfit from my new stash of clothes. Black jeans, a black and purple, lacy corset-type of thing from a rack labelled 'steampunk' and a black cardy I already owned. I put on my old Chucks which suddenly looked a whole lot cooler, and layered on a heap of necklaces.

Stepping back, I studied myself. Except I didn't

look like myself. I turned slowly in front of my mirror. My butt was still too big and I had a muffin top. Not perfect. But not all bad.

Pulling my eyes away, I surveyed the room. Pastel walls looked back at me condescendingly and the curtains were splashed with so many flowers I could almost smell them. I felt suffocated. The lamp next to my bed was pink, for crying out loud! This did not suit the new me. I was not a child. I was not invisible. I was Sylvie. And sometimes I felt crazy too.

It started in the pit of my stomach and filled out my ribcage, made me feel on the verge of exploding. I picked up my lamp and hurled it across the room. It hit the wall and fell to the ground, leaving a dent where it had made impact. Frenzied, I ripped off all the posters from my walls, pulled family photos from their frames and ripped them up, yanked the curtains so hard they partially derailed. Then I stood in the middle of the stupid, pink room and screamed.

Sometimes I felt crazy too.

Four

'Where the hell are these people?'

My room looked like it had been the subject of a home invasion and after my little episode I'd slept for a couple of hours. It was dark now and my stomach was grumbling. Still no parental presence. I couldn't ignore the angry growl of my insides anymore – I hadn't eaten anything all day.

The contents of the pantry were as follows: dried pasta, some sauces, rice, canned fruit and vegetables … So, nothing.

Pizza. I dialled the number on the fridge, but ordering was a joke – the voice-automated order system didn't understand the word 'Yes.' Useless. *One day the whole world is going to be run by incompetent robots.* Grabbing my bag, I left the house. We only lived a ten-minute walk from the village anyway. I'd just go and give my order to a human. Hopefully a human would actually make the pizza too.

The rain had cleared but the mist remained. It cast an eerie aura around the bulb of the street lights. When Calamity and I were little, we would have races to see who could sprint to the next lamp post the fastest. One time, I was in front and made the mistake of looking back at Cate to see where she was. By the time I flicked my head back around it was too late to stop, or even register what was happening, and I smacked straight into it.

That was the only time I'd ever been to hospital as a patient, and the only time I'd had my parents' full attention. Blood was gushing out of my skull – turned out I'd split it open like a melon and had a concussion. I remember spewing all over my father and the doctor shining a light into my eyes, and that's about all.

The second I was out of hospital, it was business as usual and the parents left me with Lore-liar's parents while they went to Cate's dumb recital. Lore-liar sat next to me the whole time trying to get me to play with her Barbies – *ironic much?* – but I had a thumping brain-ache and all I wanted to do was lie still on the couch and not move. And she had a little brother who was crashing around playing with Tonka trucks and watching Barney, just to make the experience even better. I burst into tears and Lore-liar's mother came in and shooed her irritating offspring out. She gave me a cuddle and brought me some more Panadol and a handful of the pikelets she'd just made. I loved Lorelei's mum. These days it baffled me that someone so nice could raise someone so hideous. I wondered if she looked at her daughter now, and felt sad. Or worse, shame.

The wind was picking up and I shivered, wishing I'd worn a coat. A car beeped as it drove past. I looked around to see what it was beeping at. All the other cars on the street were parked and the only person on the footpath was me.

A few more steps and another car came down the road. This one beeped from further away, and when it got closer a young guy was hanging out the window wolf-whistling.

At me?

Belatedly, I became aware of my changed appearance. I hadn't looked in the mirror again between waking up and leaving the house. I pulled my cardy tighter. They'd beeped and whistled at *me*.

Did that mean I looked good?

I turned and crossed the road into the village. Catching sight of myself in one of the shop windows, I saw what they saw. No way were they whistling at me. They were probably laughing about it now.

'Did you see that thing? Like she thought she was hot or something!'

They'd probably go and tell their beautiful girlfriends who would laugh at my idiocy while being showered in kisses.

The shop was warm and the lights were bright. I had to blink a couple of times while my eyes readjusted after the darkness outside. Thankfully, the staff behind the counter were not robots. I walked up to the young guy standing at the cash register and waited for him to say something. He didn't. In fact he was just standing there awkwardly. *Oh my God, is he staring at my boobs?!* I followed his gaze. Yes! If boobs could blush, mine definitely were. I resisted the urge to pull my cardy over them and cleared my throat. He snapped out of his ogling.

'Hi. Um, what would you like?'

I cleared my throat again, this time to check my voice was still there.

'Um, could I please get a mushroom and cheese pizza please?'

Ugh. What a dick.

I watched him fumble as he put through my order and took my payment. His name tag said 'Ben'.

Well if he can be that awkward, I don't have to do much to be cooler.

He handed me the change.

I forced myself to look him dead in the eye. 'Thanks, Ben.'

The tomato shade started at his neck and infused his face. I walked to a seat to wait.

A girl came in, holding hands with her boyfriend. He must have been about 18 and was wearing a leather jacket with a hood sticking out of it. They picked up their pizza and turned to leave. When he saw me, he looked for a little bit too long. His girlfriend all but hauled him out of the place. I wondered how he'd make it up to her.

This was different. I'd never been noticed so much during a ten-minute trip to the village. Maybe I wasn't pretty or thin, but I was doing something right. The hair? Or the cleavage? Whatever, I was keeping it.

'Order number 12!'

I stood up and attempted to saunter to the counter, waiting for Bashful Ben to appear with my pizza.

But it wasn't Ben.

Oh, shit. Shit, shit, shit!

The guy holding my pizza was none other than Adam Allegro. He was looking at me as if to say, *Hello? You ordered a pizza, moron.* He hadn't recognised me. But come on, the longer I left it, the more time he would have to figure it out. I looked down at my feet and ran through a list of appropriate ways to die in a pizza shop.

'Cheese and mushroom pizza?' he asked.

'Yep.'

'Better get it home fast. Don't want it to get cold …'

'Oh yeah,' I stuck out my hand and took it from him.

'Have a nice night.'

What? Adam Allegro told me to have a nice night? Like he cared? *Get a friggen grip, Sylvie. It's his job, you douche.* But I couldn't help it. I smiled! A stupid, wide, doofus-looking, head-up-and-face-meeting smile.

Something changed in Adam's face.

Crapola.

'Hey, don't you go to my school?'

I said nothing; just stared like a stunned mullet.

'You do. And you crashed into me this morning ... You look a little different now.'

His eyes were searching my face (after skimming my body). I tried to act natural.

'Well, um, I just felt like a change.'

'Sweet. Are you feeling better? You were upset, right?'

Ugh. God.

'Yeah, way better. I just didn't feel well.'

He must have heard. He thinks I like girls!

'Well. I'm glad you're up to eating a whole pizza,' he grinned.

He thinks I'm fat!

'Have a good night, Sylvie.'

Oh my freakin' God, are you kidding me?! You know my name?

'Course I do.'

Holy Huckleberry, he can read my thoughts. No. I'd said it out loud. I didn't know where to look.

'As soon as you smiled, I knew it was you.'

My eyebrows must have hit my hairline. This was too much. Was he teasing me? *Be cool.*

'I'm not a lesbian!' I blurted.

His face transformed again. Into mild surprise this time.

Oh no, he hadn't heard.

No, not surprise. Amusement.

'Okay …' he replied.

I decided to do what any other girl in the world would have done.

I bolted.

········
Five
········

'All right. It's not so bad, Sylvie,' I said, back in the safe haven of my trashed bedroom.

I'd been repeating this through mouthfuls of pizza while trying to push the entire conversation with Adam Allegro to the back of my mind. By the time I'd got home, with my protesting stomach and boxful of pizza, I'd almost convinced myself it had all been a horrifying dream. Now, though, food was in my body for the first time all day, and my brain was beginning to think straight (albeit irrationally) again. No matter how hard I tried to push them to the recesses of my mind, Adam's words kept fighting their way through.

'I'm glad you're up to eating a whole pizza.'
I'm fat.
'Have a good night, Sylvie.'
He was mocking me!

But then: 'As soon as you smiled, I knew it was you …'

What the hell is going on here?! Surely he was teasing. But what if …?

I looked down at the pizza box in front of me. It was empty. I'd devoured the entire thing.

Gross.

I did ten sit-ups to compensate, before realising that was not the best thing to do after gorging myself on what was essentially doughy bread and cheese. I needed to walk around and digest.

My hand touched the door handle just as I heard Damn-it-all Dave explode.

'What the bloody hell happened here?'

When did they get home?

He could only have been standing in the bathroom staring at the now pinkish shower. I hesitated. I could hear Pamela Panic padding down the hallway to investigate. Better own up now, I thought. They'll find out sooner or later. Taking a breath, I opened my door and walked slowly down the hall. My heart was thudding like the bass in a boy racer's car. How could I have forgotten to clean up the shower?

I stopped in the doorway to the bathroom. The parentals were standing in front of the shower muttering. Now or never.

'It was me,' I said, my voice strangely uncertain for something I was so certain about.

Their heads whipped around, and for an excruciatingly awkward second they just stared. I wondered if they knew who I was. I didn't.

My father's expression was cold. My mother was observing me, one eyebrow raised. She opened the cupboard under the sink and took out a packet of make-up remover wipes, and placed them on the vanity.

'You can clean the shower when you get home from school tomorrow, Sylvie,' she said. 'Now, take the make-up off. You don't need it. Did you find something for dinner?'

I'd been prepared for a reaction to the new Sylvie, but it still stung and I found myself suddenly dangerously close to resembling a raccoon. Stupid cheap mascara. I blinked hard and nodded mutely. My parents left.

Standing in front of the mirror, I wiped away the layers of my mask. But no amount of wiping could make the tears stop falling. I felt so small.

I showed up at school the next day wearing newly applied make-up and the black dress I'd picked up at the op shop, with a striped cropped top over it and my trusty old sneakers. I didn't usually like dresses but I was secretly hoping Adam might run into me again. I wanted him to think I was feminine, not butch. The bell rang. I steeled myself and walked into the classroom. It was humming. Eyes flicked across and then came back to rest. Silence. Apart from an exclamation of 'whoa' from one of the boys and 'oh my *God!* from one of the girls.

Lore-liar was staring at me with something like contempt on her face, when Mrs Delaney rocked up. 'Oh. I didn't realise we had a new student!' she said. 'I'm Mrs Delaney, and you are?'

Sniggers erupted around the room. My face immediately felt hot, and was probably as red as my hair.

'Um. It's me ... Sylvie?'

The woman peered at me over her glasses and then smacked herself on the forehead as if it had been perfectly obvious and she was just having a senior moment.

'Of course it's you, Sylvie! Silly me. You look a bit different.'

'That's an understatement.' This from Lore-liar. I decided then and there not to sit with her. All eyes on me, I took the seat closest to the door, hoping to make an escape as quickly as possible.

I saw him at lunchtime. I was walking to the library to meet Belle, and he appeared like some kind of vision. I'd looked all around the school at morning break but no joy. Now here he was, in all his Italian-looking hotness, walking in my direction ... sort of. He was smiling! *Oh. Not at me.* Walking by his side was Hannah Ho-bag.

The Ho-bag was probably one of the most beautiful girls you would have ever seen. She had the most glorious chocolatey brunette tresses and these freezing cold grey eyes set in coffee-coloured skin. She was like some kind of divine being. All the boys and all the girls at our school worshipped Hannah, and she had a flock of disciples that followed her around everywhere. Today, though, there was no one with her but Adam. He was listening, with his head tilted to one side and seemed to be enchanted. I didn't blame him. Adam noticed me (!) and waved vaguely in my direction before turning his attention back to the Ho-bag. She just cast me a casual look that communicated clearly what she thought of me, and pushed his shoulder gently in a way too familiar way. My heart sank as they walked past.

Seriously, Sylvie. What did you think would happen?

The library was musty and quiet. The only sounds the occasional rustling of pages. I found Belle at the computers.

'You're not doing schoolwork at lunchtime are you?'

'Yeah, I'm just printing my … why do you look like that?' She stared at me with her eyes as round as saucers behind her glasses and her mouth hanging open. Belle was another invisible person. The only thing that stood out was her nose. I actually kind of liked her nose. It had freckles splattered all over it and a bump in the bridge where her glasses sat perfectly. Glasses were cool. They added character. Bookish Belle's glasses were hugely magnified and made her hazel eyes look enormous, almost beautiful. She was a class A nerd.

'Just felt like a change.'

'Oh. Cool.' She collected her things. For all her prim geekiness, there was one thing I could always rely on Belle to be: non-judgemental. She hit print and collected her papers, then accompanied me outside where we sat on the steps with our lunches.

'I'm glad you're here today. I was worried yesterday, and for the record I don't think you're gay. Did this makeover happen yesterday?'

'Yup. Just randomly decided I didn't feel like being me anymore.'

'You'll always be you, Sylvie,' Belle said. 'The way you look doesn't change who you are.'

'Wish it did. Calamity Cate's in the psych ward again. My parents don't know I exist. And now there's rumours going around about my sexuality. Awesome. I want to be someone else.'

'Maybe you should talk to the guidance counsellor?' Belle munched on her sandwich.

'No way. She's useless.'

'No she's not. I went to her once.'

My apple fell out of my hand. 'What?'

'I went to the guidance counsellor,' she repeated calmly for the mentally slow one of our duo. 'I went because I was feeling too stressed about schoolwork and it was affecting my whole life. She helped.'

'But that's totally different! Don't you think being stressed about schoolwork is a little bit different to having parents who ignore you because your sister is in a psych ward again after trying to commit suicide for the hundredth time?'

Bookish Belle's expression transformed into something that could only be described as stony.

'Well, I'm sorry, Sylvie, to hear that your life is so hard. Maybe you've never heard of relativity, and that's a shame because you'll have trouble getting through life assuming that your own trauma is so much worse than everyone else's. I hope the "new you" – *she said this with inverted commas!* – 'makes the old you feel better.' This entire mini monologue was spoken so quietly I actually got goosebumps.

I didn't even have time to react before she picked up her bag and stalked back into the library. Great. I spent the rest of the lunch hour sitting by myself, reeling at how judgemental non-judgemental Belle of the Books had just been.

Six

I knelt by the shower scrubbing the floor and walls with a rag soaked in bleach. The red was coming out quite nicely, and it gave me an unexpected sense of satisfaction. Satisfaction from cleaning? Maybe I should've been the one in a mental health unit.

I'd arrived home to find a note from Pamela informing me that she and Dave had gone to visit Cate again, and would be home for dinner if I could throw something together please. This was next to a bottle of bathroom bleach which promised me it would clean any bathroom surface. Surprisingly, I managed to scrub that shower in record time, and when I was done I flicked through channels to see what was on TV. Pretty much nothing.

An ad came on depicting a son cooking a delicious meal for his parents, showing what you can make if you shop at Foodmart on the cheap. I sat up, inspired. Maybe my parents would appreciate me if I put on a nice dinner for them.

The kitchen actually contained some nice food for once. Pamela must have been shopping. Rummaging through the items, I pulled out some spinach, capsicums and mushrooms and threw them on the chopping board. Standing on tip-toes, I grasped a can of tinned tomatoes and some fettuccine.

As the chopped vegetables were frying, I threw fettuccine into a pot of boiling water. I didn't follow recipes. One thing I had actually always been good at was creative cooking. In recent days, though, our family seemed to live on takeaways or boring war rations like Nana talks about: boiled veggies and sausages. I poured the tinned tomatoes and juice into the pan with the veggies and added some cream. The cream mingled with the tomato juice and turned a pinkish shade. In went the salt and pepper and some Italian herb mixture.

I was carrying the dish to the table, imagining myself as the demure picture of virtue, when my father rumbled into the kitchen, went straight up to the fridge and took out a beer. My mother followed. She was red with fury. It was pretty clear they'd been fighting.

'I made dinner …' I said.

She was staring at him with an expression I couldn't recognise. Sometimes I thought adult faces showed so much more emotion than young faces because they had feelings young people hadn't felt yet. Her eyes took in the dinner table and her features softened. *Because of me?*

'Thanks, Sylvie, that smells delicious.'

My father looked like a statue. I could only see his profile, but his jaw was clenching and unclenching and he was looking straight ahead, at nothing, as if in a trance.

'Yeah, thanks, girl. Did you clean the shower?'

'Yes, good as new.'

'Good. You need to take that crap off your face.'

'Would you even notice if I did?'

He didn't respond.

After dinner, I escaped to the kitchen and made a hot chocolate. There was an open bottle of Baileys on the bench. My mother had a penchant for a glass of Baileys with her dinner, especially after a hard day. Carefully, quietly, I unscrewed the lid and poured some into my hot chocolate. I'd seen her do it before. One sip. It was like velvet in my throat. On a whim, I tipped my hot chocolate down the sink and filled the whole mug with Baileys. I took it to my room and closed my eyes, sipping the smooth velvetiness. It was like a milkshake.

My parents were arguing in the lounge. I didn't know what about and I didn't want to. They didn't appreciate the effort I put into cooking for them and they hadn't even bothered to ask how my day was. *As usual.* Tomorrow was Friday, and for that I was extremely grateful given the fact that I had zero friends to talk to. The sips of alcohol turned into gulps and I was beginning to feel nice and relaxed. I hadn't realised how much tension was in my back until it started to melt away. In fact, all my muscles started to feel nice and fuzzy and the world began to be bearable. I fell asleep to the sound of my parents bickering.

When I woke up there was a funny taste in my mouth, and the muscles that had been so nice and slack when I went to sleep, were tight and knotty again as I reached out to turn off my alarm.

In the shower, the water was hot to the point of nearly unbearable, but I let it manipulate my back and neck while I tried not to think about the day ahead. When I got out of the shower, my skin was bright pink. I pulled on a short black dress with lace peeking out from under the hem and surveyed myself in the mirror. Too much black. I snuck down the hall, past my bedroom, to Calamity's room and opened her drawer full of miscellaneous items, selecting a red silk scarf to tie around my waist. It looked good if I didn't breathe.

School dragged. I had no one to hang out with and I knew people were talking about me. I elected to keep my head down and focus on work. I wrote the crap out of an essay about teen pregnancy, and at lunchtime I sat in the corner of a classroom by myself and doodled on my books. Some of the nerds were there, too, doing schoolwork, and a guy by the name of Chris who had to stay behind and copy out the dictation he'd been caught not doing during the lesson. Chris was one of the 'popular' ones. In fact, I thought Lore-liar had a crush on him at one stage. He was tall and good-looking, if you liked buzz-cuts and arrogant smiles, and was a friend of Adam's – they were in the same cricket team.

I was pretty confident that I had gone unnoticed by everyone in my little corner when a paper dart hit me square in the skull and floated gracefully to the floor. I picked it up and looked around the room for the culprit.

Chris was packing up his things, looking at me and grinning.

Guilty.

He kicked back his chair and slouched out of the room, having probably written all the dictation using text abbreviations. I touched my phone to text Belle about it, but quickly remembered our spat. I'd run out of room on my books to doodle and opened up the dart to continue scrawling on it. Something was written there: 'You're cute. Come to my party next Saturday.'

Holy. Shit.

I didn't know what was more exciting. The fact that this Chris, who I didn't even like but was popular, thought I was cute, or the fact that Adam would probably be at his party too. I read and reread the note until the bell rang. Getting any schoolwork done for the rest of the afternoon was a joke. I was still dying to text Belle, but didn't want to be the one to grovel. I wondered what she'd say.

Seven

The weekend was its own form of hell. I'd managed to contract the plague and ended up lying in bed feeling sorry for myself. My head felt like a steamroller had bowled right over it and my throat was sandpaper. I couldn't lie down for fear of death by snot obstruction, but if I sat up my nose ran like a tap. I wasn't the type that got sick often, so every time I did I realised I'd forgotten how hideous it was. I looked repulsive. A jersey was flung over the mirror so I didn't have to see myself. I was pretty sure I was dying.

The upside to the plague was that my mother actually showed some motherly feelings towards me. She set me up in bed and wheeled in the TV from her room. She bought me cups of lemon and honey drink, and gave me panadol for my hammering headache and sore throat. She made sure I had a neverending supply of tissues and even made me chicken noodle soup. Most amazingly of all, she didn't go and see Cate once.

'Not while my other girl's sick' she said, dumping a bunch of trashy magazines on my bed. 'It's times like these a girl needs her mum.'

I smiled and relaxed my tired shoulders. 'Thanks.'

I meant it too.

She paused in the doorway and returned the smile. 'And anyway, I can't go to the hospital with germs.'

I felt too unwell to question her about why she felt the need to add that onto the end of what was, for us, a warm and fuzzy mother-daughter moment.

I could hear Pamela pottering around in the kitchen preparing another batch of soup. I flicked through the magazines she'd bought me and hugged my old teddy, Valentina Violet, wishing the cold would go away soon. I was too young to die. In my snot-filled haze, it occurred to me that perhaps Pamela Panic was the type of woman who needed someone to look after. Maybe she needed to feel needed, and that's what I was doing wrong.

I knew the type, Lore-liar's mother was a bit like that, and probably every nurse in the world was too. They were the ones who fronted up when everyone else was falling to bits and losing their minds with worry. Maybe my mother's panicky trait was just a desperate need to fulfil her true calling, even though she possibly didn't even know it herself.

My mother bustled back in with a bowl of steaming soup, minestrone this time, which I was sure would've smelt incredible had my olfactory system not been bunged up. She'd even made soldiers! With heaps of butter. Just how I used to like them when I was little.

As I sipped my soup and dunked the soldiers, she tapped away on her laptop in the lounge. Probably finishing off her latest article before the *Women's World* went to print. I wondered if Cate's illness was her secret shame. Did her friends know about it, or did she keep it under wraps? '*My oldest has gone away to a health camp, but my second is still at home. Yes, yes, Dave and I are very lucky to have such wonderful girls …*'

Did they know that she and my father slept in separate bedrooms? Did adults talk about that kind of thing? When Mum's friends used to come over for coffee, I'd eavesdrop on their conversations. It was easy to listen from the top of the stairs in our old house. I got the impression that adults tended to discuss everything but the difficult topics, as opposed to teenagers who focused only on the hard stuff. I wondered at what age a person found the right balance.

Anyway, since we'd moved her friends didn't come around anymore. Neither did mine.

I lifted my heavy head and looked at the clock. Twelve o'clock. Cate would be having lunch most likely. She was in the adult ward these days and, to be honest, I didn't like going to visit her there. This was her second admission to that unit. Mostly people watched TV or stayed in their rooms, but sometimes you'd hear them charging down the halls yelling about something or other. They'd stride past you with an army of staff members behind them.

I felt vulnerable there. Sometimes I thought they could tell how I was feeling – like mental illness was some kind of magic affliction. It was in the way they looked at me. Cate was better and nearing discharge when I whispered this to her. She laughed 'You sound paranoid!'

I shut up about it after that because I didn't want to end up in there, ever. On my first visit, I'd been rattled by a man wearing a towel on his head like a turban as he sprinted into the TV room and announced the time had come for us all to die and be reincarnated as pot plants. An old woman scuttled up to me and took my hand. Her hair was slick with gel and she reeked of cigarettes.

'Don't be afraid, love,' she said kindly. 'That's just Greg; you've got to put him in his place.' She then proceeded to yell abuse at Greg until the staff ushered them both out of the room.

Indignant, I turned to Cate who was looking at me with amusement. 'I'm not scared.'

'Yes, you are. The people here can be very perceptive, but,' she leaned closer, as if sharing with me the secret to the universe, 'your feelings show pretty clearly on your face.'

I spent all that evening trying to master an impassive expression in the mirror.

Eight

I had to take Monday and Tuesday off school. After being doted on for four days I had to admit I was a little melancholic about feeling so much better. I tried to milk it for another day, but my mother came into my room, took one look at me and proclaimed my miraculous recovery. She was going to interview some celebrity who'd had a baby, she told me, and then would see Cate. She informed me that she wouldn't be taking me in case I coughed or something, even though it was more than obvious that I wouldn't want to go and see my sister anyway.

'Yes, Mum,' I mumbled as I grabbed my bag and ducked out the door.

She followed me to the steps. 'I wish you wouldn't wear that make-up, Sylvie.'

'I know.'

'Have a good day.'

'Yip.'

'Oh, hold on a minute, love.' She disappeared into the depths of the house, returning momentarily waving a ten dollar note at me.

'Money for dinner tonight. Don't spend it on your way home!' She tried to sweep my hair back and I ducked.

'I'll miss the bus!' I left her standing on the front steps in her floral dressing gown, winding her dark blonde hair around her finger.

Having no friends these days, I had expected that no one would miss me. School carried on as it always had, regardless of whether or not I was alive or dead. I stayed behind to ask nicely for an extension from Mrs Delaney at lunchtime, and after negotiating over the date and winning, I walked out into the hall, feeling quite proud of myself.

Behind me, a cleared throat, and then, 'Sylvie.'

Chris was walking towards me, half smiling and shifty-eyed. He looked like someone who was always up to something. I'd pushed Friday's happenings to the back of my mind while I was suffering the Black Death, but when I saw his face it hit me like a tidal wave.

'Where've you been?'

'What?' I couldn't have heard him right.

'You were away,' he said slowly, as if talking to a child. A stupid child. His face broke into a grin that was all untrustworthy mischief.

'You weren't wagging were you?'

Hmm, what to tell him … I could deny the allegations and tell him the truth – that I was lying in bed, filled up with snot and cuddling my teddy, or …

'Yup,' I made a quick decision. 'Just decided Dr Phil looked more interesting than English and maths.'

He laughed. *He laughed?!* I was funny? Was it that easy?

'Rebel.'

I said nothing, deciding it was the safer option.

'I hope you can make my party on Saturday. Give me your number and I'll text you the where and when.'

Holy. Huckleberry.

'Um yup okay sure … I'll just have to find my phone, oh no, I don't need to find it cos you're going to take my number so I don't even need it anyway …' I was rambling. Chris was putting my name into his phone and raised his eyebrows at me briefly. I was officially probably the biggest spaz that ever lived. I got my number out in the correct order and made a hasty exit before I could betray my 'coolness' again.

Arriving home to an empty house, I lay on the couch and went over things in my head. I absolutely could not believe that Chris had my number in his phone. This was a guy I had barely even noticed before. He was so under my radar that I didn't even have a nickname for him! A thought struck me like a bolt of lightning and I sat up with an impending sense of doom.

What if it was all a joke? What if he was going to start pranking me, or laughing behind my back with Adam and Hannah Ho-bag? Lore-liar had recently been initiated into that group too. How would she react to me being invited to this party? I ruminated on this for way too long and was roused out of my mounting anxieties when my phone beeped. Instinctively I knew who it was. I had no friends, so who else could it be? My heart started fluttering in my chest and my hands went all jittery. An unrecognised number.

> Hey, party's at 87 Palliser ave starts 7 where something hot ☺

Okay, so I willed myself to overlook the fact that he was grammatically challenged and focussed on the 'hot'. I'd have to borrow something of Cate's. Not so much to look hot for Chris, but it was imperative that I looked hot for Adam.

'Adam!' I said aloud into the empty room.

If Chris had missed me, maybe Adam would've too. There was one way to find out. Without thinking, I snatched up my bag and rushed out in the direction of the pizza shop.

It was November and the spring weather was getting up my nose. I never knew what to wear when the forecast was always wrong and the weather was bipolar. It was a clear, sunny day; a day that appeared warm but was actually freezing. In my head I jotted down a note to purchase a jacket that suited my new look and just about jumped out of my skin when a passing car beeped its frickin' horn at me again. It made me self-conscious (even more than I already was), because I had no idea if they were communicating that I looked good, or if my skirt was hitched halfway up my butt.

Whilst attempting to subtly check the decency of my skirt, I ran through scenarios in my head of how things would pan out when I saw Adam. Bracing myself against the cold and the potential complete rejection that was probably more likely than any of the romantic ideas that had just danced across my mind, I pushed the door to the shop to enter, which would've been a lot more successful if it hadn't been a pull door. As it happened, I'd thrust my chest out, done my best trout pout and smacked straight into it. Classy.

Throwing a glance around to make sure no one had noticed, I flicked my hair, *pulled* the door, and entered. My heart shrivelled. Adam Allegro was nowhere to be seen. Bashful Ben was behind the counter, red and grinning shyly, while apparently doing everything in his power to avoid eye contact. I dragged my feet up to the counter, placed my order for the usual and sat down on the bench to wait. I pretended to flick through a magazine, trying not to let my disappointment get the better of me. But seriously, I thought, as I snapped a page over a little violently, *of course* this is what would happen to me.

The bone-chilling air attacked my back as the door opened and I shivered, also a little more violently than was strictly necessary.

'Sylvie!'

I dropped the magazine, all class, and whipped around. 'Adam Allegro!'

'That's my name,' he laughed, and his eyes twinkled like fairy lights.

I wondered if I'd finally lost my marbles. I came over all giddy and giggly, resorting to biting my lip and staring at the ceiling while regaining composure.

Composure? Who am I kidding? I'm in the presence of a deity.

'Pizza again?'

He had the prettiest smile I'd ever seen.

'When you weren't here I thought I'd got away with it.'

'Busted. My shift's just started. But I'm a fellow pizza appreciator so I support your passion.'

'Oh, well, yeah, my mum isn't home a lot these days so she leaves me money for takeaways. Pizza is my first choice. Obviously.'

Hold on. What had I just told him? *Too much info.*

'I mean, y'know, she is home sometimes but she just has to go and see my sister. With my dad. She goes with my dad.'

Way to go, screwball.

'Where's your sister?'

Oh, shit. She's in another city? She's in space? She's on

Shortland Street? *What to say, what to say?*

'She's in hospital,' I replied lamely.

'Oh that's too bad, I hope she's okay?' He said it in a searching way, as if he was asking a question. His face held what looked like actual concern.

'Yeah, she'll be fine. She's just got, um,' *think quick, think quick!* 'diabetes.'

Really? Good one, Sylvie.

'That's no good.'

Okay way too much caring for Cate here folks. How to turn it around …

'Yeah. So did you miss me?' *Woah, too forward!*

He looked perplexed. Perplexed was never good.

'Miss you?'

A small cough, a giggle. 'Just kidding,' *Not.* 'I've been away for a couple of days.'

'Yeah? Me too. Had a cold.'

'Me too!' This from me, a little too enthusiastically.

'Two people with springtime colds? We must be a rarity,' he smiled and leaned in conspiratorially. 'Maybe people will think we gave it to each other.'

This was followed by a wink, me quietly dying inside, and my order being called.

'See ya later,' he said easily, as I all but skipped towards the door.

'Yeah, see ya.' I pulled the push door.

Yeah. Classy.

Nine

The sweltering afternoon sun had taken the edge off the water but goosebumps still erupted all over my skin. I strode out into the beckoning expanse of ocean until it hugged my waist. With a glance back to my belongings waiting patiently on the sand, I lay on the water letting my feet glide up with the buoyancy, and allowed the wise old sea to carry me.

I'd arrived home from school in a good mood, pleased with my new found popularity. I stupidly assumed that my mother and I were still on warm and fuzzy terms, and so was surprised when she interrupted my animated chatter by spinning around, throwing her glasses on the desk and exploding at me.

'For the love of God, Sylvia, are you ever going to ask how your sister is?!'

There was a brief silence as I stared at her in shock

and tried to gather enough words to form a coherent sentence in my defence.

'I assumed you would tell me if there was something I needed to know,' I said, carefully.

'You assume a lot of things these days don't you?'

Harsh.

I felt like she'd ripped off the top layer of my skin. It wasn't often that my guard was down in the first place, now I remembered why. I felt so angry and attacked, humiliated that I had ever assumed – *there I go again* – that my mother would actually want to hear about my day. It was all I could do not to cry.

At the time I wasn't sure where I was going, but as soon as the bus pulled up at the beach I had a feeling I'd known all along. When Cate was well, this was our place. We used to go swimming together all the time. The sight of the sun glittering on the surface, the salty smell carried my way by the breeze, the sound of the ocean lapping the sand, had the same effect as a rejuvenating back massage.

I felt alive.

I hadn't come prepared for swimming, but the water had always been this irresistible force for Cate and me; it seemed as if it contained a magnet in its depths and every time it crept up and enveloped the sand, it would pull us closer on its way back out. Before I knew it I was wriggling out of my jeans. I could taste the saltwater before I even reached the waves. It kissed my knees as I waded further out, and lifted me up as though my burdens weren't so heavy after all. It was so reliable, our sea.

With an uninterrupted opportunity to reflect, I wondered if Pamela Panic had a valid reason to be mad at me. Although I did care about how Calamity Cate was doing, it wasn't like we hadn't been through all this before. While there was the part of me that cared, there was a part of me that totally didn't want to face it. Surely my mother should've been able to recognise that? Maybe I wasn't dealing with it that well, but she was the adult and I was the child and it was wrong of her to be such a bitch to me. I decided I had no reason to forgive her, and anyway, did Cate ever ask the parentals how *I* was doing?

As if. She was too busy being crazy.

I remembered a time when Cate was in the initial stages of her illness. Her moods were all over the place and she'd started having what the parentals assured themselves were 'nightmares'. At the worldly age of 12, even I had identified this as a glaring untruth – how could Cate be having nightmares when she never *slept?* She said she saw a little girl in her room, and was convinced she'd killed her and this was her ghost coming to haunt her. When she told me this I had no idea how to react so I took the route the adults were taking.

'It was just a dream Catie,' I tried to explain, in a gentle but superior tone, as if I knew what I was talking about. 'Y'know, the ones that people have over and over again. The girl isn't real …' I trailed off.

She was looking at me suspiciously. I knew I was wading into waters too deep for me. She met my eye and said conversationally, 'Maybe I'm dreaming now and you're not real.'

In that moment she gave me a glimpse of what it felt like to live inside her head.

What if I ended up like her?

'It's not real, Cate. Mum and Dad say it's not real.' I thought I'd won the argument until Cate came back with, 'Well don't come running to me when you find the demons under your bed too.'

Well that was awesome.

Even now I would always check under my bed before I climbed in at night. Here I was, 15, checking for demons under my bed, and scared to death that I would follow in Calamity Cate's footsteps. For about two months after my birthday I had seriously questioned the state of my own mental health. Everyone in the world has weird brain randomness sometimes. The mind is a confusing place. Most people would brush the odd mind warp off, but to me, they became early warning signs.

Once, an internet site that I was on had some kind of error and when I typed in words they came out backwards. I hit backspace and retried it about 20 times, each time becoming more and more convinced I was having a psychotic episode. I ended up getting super distressed and called in my father to confirm what I was seeing.

He grunted. 'Site must be malfunctioning,' he said, before walking out again.

I'd spent five minutes after he left the room taking deep breaths and trying to slow my racing heart.

The sun was beginning to make its slow descent. Reluctantly I made my way back to the shore. Once out of the water, I sprinted to my clothes and tugged on my jeans even though my legs were still wet. Ugh. With the sun hiding it was frickin' freezing. I wondered if my parents would be there when I got home. I boarded the bus, wishing it would crash and kill everyone on board – *actually, just me would be fine* – so that they might actually notice me. And by then it would be too late. Although it wouldn't really make me feel any better since I would be dead and not even around to see.

They were home. Damn-it-all Dave was watching a documentary and doing his daily newspaper crossword. This was the closest to multitasking he ever got. Pamela Panic was ironing. She swooped on me when I walked in the door and followed me to my room.

'I saved you some dinner. I made enchiladas they're your favourite aren't they?'

'I'm not hungry.' I opened my door.

'I'm sorry I yelled at you, honey. I'm just a bit stressed …' She looked at me searchingly, sheepishly.

'Aren't we all, Mother! And by the way, how *is* Cate?'

She didn't have a chance to reply. I slammed the door in her stupid face.

Ten

The remainder of the week consisted of studying for exams and avoiding Belle and Lorelei, which wasn't too difficult since they were obviously determined to avoid me too.

I sat in the far corner of the room in every class and kept my head down. I avoided the library because I knew that's where Belle would be, opting instead to stay behind in class to study or find a spare room at the student learning centre. I wasn't expecting to do well in exams – I was just aiming to pass. I figured the better my grades, the higher the chance I could pick up a job somewhere, or get into a polytech. Then I'd be free to leave my parents and go flatting. A bit of a stretch and in the back of my mind I knew it wouldn't be that easy, but it was what kept me chugging along and I wasn't prepared to let reality stain it.

I was halfway to the Learning Centre, distracted by trying to locate my cellphone in my bag, when a voice said 'Hey, Sylvie.'

My eyes flicked around, past Hannah Ho-bag because obviously she wouldn't be talking to me, and then back to Hannah Ho-bag as it became apparent that she was the only one around.

Huh?

Her eyes moved over me slowly. I bet she wants to copy my homework, I thought, completely brushing aside the fact that apart from being Miss Popularity 2014 and looking like a supermodel, she was actually really smart.

I felt that was more than a little unfair. Some people get Karen Walker genes, some people get Warehouse genes.

'I hear you're coming to Chris's party.' She sauntered towards me. The breeze made her hair flutter and I was struck with this bizarre thought that she'd dragged me into a Pantene commercial.

Act natural.

'Yeah I guess I am.'

Did that come across as non-committal or not all there? It was so hard trying to speak 'popular'. She smiled in a distracted way and her eyes glittered with … what? Excitement? Malice? I wasn't sure.

'Sweet. See you there,' she nearly frickin' purred, and catwalked away.

What just happened?

I found a spare room in the Learning Centre but I couldn't concentrate. I ended up googling 'hot party outfits' and spent the majority of lunch time poring through images of beautiful skinny girls who could've worn a paperbag and looked good. These sites were made for people like Hannah, not people like me. Karen Walker genes, not Warehouse. I resolved to go home and raid my sister's wardrobe. She was bound to have something 'hot' in there somewhere.

What did that word even mean? Did it mean beautiful, or did beautiful go out the window in favour of revealing? Was I supposed to wear a short skirt and low-cut top, leaving nothing to the imagination, or would I look better in something I was comfortable in? Did my own personal comfort even enter the equation at all? I had a feeling it didn't. The bell rang, roughly pushing me out of my pondering and after a mild panic that I'd done no study I collected my stuff and went to class.

I was still preoccupied with what to wear during the last period of the day, when it occurred to me that I hadn't even told my parents what my plans were. Would they let me go? As soon as the bell rang I escaped; trying to catch the early bus so I could jam study, wardrobe-raiding and parent dealings into my evening.

No one was home when I got there. There was no money on the table either, which told me they must have been planning on being around for dinner. No pizza tonight then. I pushed open the door to my sister's room.

It felt empty and still. Cold too.

I got a chill as I walked from the doorway to her dressing table. In a way, it was like Cate had died. The room had an air of emptiness, even though it was filled with Cate's belongings. Things she loved, things she wore, things she collected, things that smelt of her. Her bed was unmade; exactly as it had been when I walked into her room what seemed like ages ago but was only a couple of weeks, and found her unconscious.

This room felt like it belonged to someone who was no longer around, and who no longer loved it or anything it contained. And in a way that was true.

I shivered again and winged a silent prayer to 'whoever' that she was safe.

See? I did care.

Rummaging through her clothes I unrolled a deep red camisole and a packet of cigarettes fell at my feet. I picked it up. It had five cigarettes and a tiny lighter tucked inside.

I didn't even know Cate smoked.

I dropped the packet on her bed and when I raised my gaze I found myself looking at the photographs stuck to Cate's wall with Blu Tack. There were some of her and her old friends. Like me, she didn't really have any friends now. She'd burnt her bridges. Our bridges. The majority of the photos were of the two of us. I climbed onto her bed and sat by the wall looking at them all.

I couldn't tell whether I was happy or sad. Bitter-sweet? There was the photo of us as little kids at Dreamworld in Australia. Cate had eaten too much candyfloss and popcorn and threw it up all over the place about five minutes post-photo. I was wearing a pink sunhat and had my arm around her, beaming. Her smile was beginning to fade and she was holding her stick of candyfloss out to our father who was standing out of shot.

There was a photo of us when I was ten and Cate was thirteen, on our grandparents' yacht on Christmas Day. We were both unwrapping our presents from them and received the same things: a beautiful bracelet from Turkey and a leather wallet from Italy. Mine was silvery grey with flowers embroidered on it; Cate's was turquoise with birds. Best Christmas ever.

We'd spent the whole summer on the yacht and sailed from the Coromandel to the Whitsundays in Australia. We would escape to a little corner up on deck and lie on our stomachs, watching the ripples and waves of the ocean as the boat sliced through it. Just Cate and me, with our beloved sea.

On one of the bedposts on Cate's bed hung a wire crown. It was mine. Dave had made one each for both of us when we were younger, but in typical absent-minded fashion, Cate had lost hers and then tried to tell me that the one I was wearing on my head was *hers.* I had to wear it for a full week and hide it in my T-shirt drawer at night to stop her from stealing it. I liked that I was the only one wearing the crown, for once. I put it on now and stared at myself in the mirror.

Who should rightfully wear the crown? Both sisters had fallen from grace.

I turned my attention back to the clothes, wriggling into a tight pink boob tube which almost cut my circulation off and forced grotesque rolls of fat to spill out over the top. *Are you serious? I even have armpit fat!* A great look with the crown.

Eventually I settled on a deep purple skirt which reached my mid-thigh and a lacy black singlet. I discovered a little black cropped cardy with black sequins at the bottom of one of her drawers. I so wished that my sister was there and well and able to give me big sisterly advice on how to present myself and how to behave.

Gathering up the pile of clothes, I headed for the door and as my hand touched the handle I caught a glimpse of something yellow out of the corner of my eye. I found myself looking at the poster for Amnesty International which was hanging on her wall above her bookcase: *Better to light a candle than curse the darkness.* Now I knew why her Facebook status had seemed so familiar.

I'd laid the outfit on the chair in my room with the crown on top and was sitting on the bed studying when I heard the front door open and Pamela's heels click-clacking on the floor. There was a rap on my door.

'Are you in there, girl?' Dave. 'Fish and chips for dinner. Better be quick if you want some.'

'Okay.' I replied. 'And for the record I wish we didn't have takeaways so much.'

'Rubbish. A real teenager would never say that.'

Touché.

Afterwards, I cleared up all the greasy papers and put away the tomato and tartare sauces. I stood in the lounge doorway awkwardly. The parents both turned their attention to me, quiet and expectant.

'Um, there's this party on Saturday and – .'

'No.' This from Damn-it-all Dave; he turned back to the TV.

Pamela Panic glanced at me, a tight smile and a shrug, and went back to her book.

Fury burst inside me from depths I didn't even know existed.

'Why not?!' I cried, fists balled at my side, my whole body rigid and dramatically increasing in temperature.

'Because I said.'

'I'll be good!'

'No, Sylvia, you are 15 years old. You're supposed to be studying for exams, not going out to parties.'

I went off like a rocket. My hand flew out and whacked the door frame. Pamela Panic froze. I froze.

Damn-it-all Dave heaved himself up off the couch.

'That is enough!' He roared. 'Go to your room. I don't want to see your face for the rest of the night.'

I spun around and ran to my room, slamming the door so hard the neighbours probably thought they felt an earthquake.

Eleven

Chris found me on Friday in the Learning Centre, bent over my books, writing and highlighting facts about the Anzacs. I had this down. History was my thing. I was so immersed in textbooks and flashcards that I didn't even notice when he pulled a chair out and sat down next to me.

'Hello?' he said, tapping my shoulder.

Being a jumpy, nervous idiot, I just about went through the roof, pulling my arm back in surprise and swiftly knocking all of my highlighters off the table. Laughing, he bent and picked one up for me. I took it with trembling fingers and stared at him.

'How did you know I'd be here?'

'Because you're always here. What are you studying?'

'History.'

'Huh. I haven't started studying yet. I'm hoping

my good looks will get me through.' He grinned.

I supressed a cringe. *What a dick*, I thought, before quickly reminding myself I needed to stop thinking, given my tendency to speak thoughts aloud.

His fingers rapped the tabletop as his eyes scanned my colourfully highlighted notes. I felt those stupid cheeks flush again and shut my books

'Colours help me learn,' I said.

Seriously? Colours help me learn? Like, I'm three and watching Play School? *Awesome, Sylvie Rivers. Just awesome.*

'… So, will I be seeing you tomorrow night?' he asked, evidently deciding it was not a good idea to carry on a conversation about schoolwork with a repulsive nerd.

'Uh, actually, I might not be able to make it …'

'Oh what?! Why not? It's gonna go off.'

'Yeah, yeah, I'd like to go but y'know … Just stuff's come up …'

He looked at me suspiciously.

'I hope it's not just that your olds said no.'

Gah! Can he see right through me?

He pushed back his chair and stood up.

'Because most people's parents always say no. But they always sneak out and come.'

I looked up at him. I hadn't thought of that.

'Well, then what do your parents think of it all?'

He laughed and turned to leave.

'They're out of town,' he said over his shoulder.

I watched him walk away and then turned back to my study. Could I do that? Was I brave enough? Or was it more a case of being stupid enough? The words in front of me blurred as my attention was completely taken up by this revelation.

All day Saturday I was distracted and jittery. I couldn't make up my mind whether or not I was brave enough or stupid enough to try and sneak out. Chris's place was a fairly long bus ride away. What if I chickened out on the bus? What if I got into trouble and needed to be picked up? What if I got in trouble and got brought home by the cops? What if I needed my mum?

The outfit I'd picked out of Cate's wardrobe was still laid out over my chair. I could've sworn the sequins were winking at me. I had a feeling I'd look nice in it. I wanted to look nice for Adam. What if he was there and I wasn't and he ended up being brainwashed by that Ho-bag seductress? That's if he hadn't already.

I'd told my parents I was going to be holed up in my room the whole night studying. Damn-it-all Dave nodded approvingly and patted the top of my head, telling me he expected to see good grades. Pamela Panic told me they were going to see Calamity and then going to a work function for Dave and wouldn't be home til late.

Are these people demented? They either had a lot of faith that I wouldn't sneak out to the party which had, a couple of nights ago, created World War III in their house, or they were as stupid as me.

Or maybe, they just don't care after all.

Six o'clock rolled around. I still hadn't made up my mind but I was so preoccupied with it that any attempts at study were futile. At 6:20 I gave in to temptation and tried on the outfit that had been sitting patiently on my chair. I felt kind of pretty. The clothes fitted me in all the right places and the purple skirt was so nice, the way it fell around my thighs. I even had cleavage, God forbid. I blushed at my own reflection. That sort of started the ball rolling and I picked up my cheap makeup to experiment with a 'smokey eye' that I'd read about online. I straightened my hair with Cate's straighteners and appraised the end result in the mirror again.

I couldn't believe this was me. Overcome with excitement at my transformation, I squealed (yes, squealed) and clapped my hands in delight. My phone buzzed. I knew who it was without looking.

Chris: Hey, u comin?

Feeling brave I smiled at my reflection, and she smiled back.

Me: Yup, c u soon

Butterflies came alive in my stomach as I grabbed my bag and ran down to the bus stop.

Twelve

The bus ride was long and I thought I was going to explode. I could barely contain my excitement and had this ridiculous urge to text Bookish Belle and tell her where I was going. I hoped she'd be jealous, although deep down I knew she wouldn't be. She just didn't care about popularity. But whatever. Maybe one day I'd be happily married to Adam Allegro and she'd be a boring librarian. *Sylvie Allegro*, I whispered in my head. *I'm Sylvie Allegro.* Inside I was positively fizzing.

I went over scenarios in my head of what would happen at the party. I imagined he'd see me across the room and his mouth would drop open. He'd make his way over to me and say, *You're beautiful*, and for once in my life I'd think it might be true. Then we'd dance for a while and go for a walk up to the lookout near Chris's street. There we would laugh and talk about our dreams and watch the sunrise. Which is when he would kiss me and tell me he loved me. I could hear his voice in my head. *I love you, Sylvie Rivers. Let's run away together.*

I smiled to myself (at least, I hoped it was to myself) and felt light-headed as I pushed the buzzer for the bus to stop. When it did, I jumped out and took a steadying breath. The night was warm and still. And it was going to be amazing.

When I knocked on the door of Chris's architecturally astounding house, no one came. Was I too early? What if it was a joke? What if they ignored me all night? I turned to gap it but people were walking up the path towards me. I couldn't leave now, it would look weird.

'Hey,' one of them said to me.

It was two guys and two girls. One of the girls had deep red hair with ringlets and skin like a china doll. She was wearing a Sex Pistols T-shirt and jeans. The other one was wearing layered singlets and a ragged looking cardigan. The boys were in jeans and T-shirts. I felt overdressed. The group looked at me quizzically.

'Um, hi,' I managed. 'No one's coming to the door, so …'

'So you open it,' Red Ringlets replied as her boyfriend turned the handle.

'Oh.' I fell into line behind them. They were carrying wine and beer bottles.

Oh jeez, I hadn't thought of bringing alcohol.

I hadn't thought of bringing anything! Should I have brought chippies? Asparagus rolls? They'd obviously been there before. I followed them as they walked confidently into a room that was packed with people and were swarmed by another bunch of party-goers. Already popular. Already confident.

What the hell am I doing here? The room was filled with people from school. Some of them glanced my way with interest, skimmed what I was wearing and went back to their conversations. I was relieved to see that the levels of dress were mixed. I figured I must have fallen somewhere in the middle of the gradient. Every person in the room was holding an alcoholic beverage.

A strong grip caught my arm. Adam. I turned around to meet his beautiful eyes. No. It was Chris. My heart sank.

'You're not thinking of leaving are you?' He smiled lazily. Was he already drunk? His breath smelt of beer and I got a whiff of musky sweat as he flung his arm around my shoulders and guided me to a group standing by a giant open window, smoking. I was pretty super anti-cigarettes but what they were smoking had a different smell. I wondered if it was weed.

The group turned to me en masse and some of the girls started giggling. *Why?* I recoiled, but Chris's arm tightened around my shoulders.

'Don't worry, they're all stoned,' he laughed.

I wasn't sure why that was funny. He took me around and introduced me to everyone.

'This is Sylvie.'

'Meet my friend, Sylvie.'

'Guys, say hello to Sylvie.'

I allowed him to lead me awkwardly through the introductions with a series of small waves, hugs from strangers and a chorus of hellos, all the while scanning the place for Adam. He didn't appear to be there. A girl approached me, stumbling a little.

'Have the rest of my wine,' she slurred, holding out her half-full glass for me to take. 'I'm pissed and you're way too sober.' Her eye make-up had smudged so she resembled a panda.

Since it would be rude to refuse, I took the glass and thanked her. One sip. It felt tangy on my tongue and made my mouth water involuntarily. I squeezed my eyes shut and took some more gulps. My tummy rumbled. I hadn't thought about dinner. Hannah Hobag appeared in front of me. *Well, at least she's not with Adam.* To my surprise, she pulled me into a hug. She smelt strongly of vanilla perfume and alcohol.

'Sylvie!' she cried. 'I've been waiting for you to get here.'

'You have?'

She looked incredible. Her eyes were glittering with this shimmery eyeshadow and her skin was glowing. Her hair was piled into some sort of elaborate up-do, which must have had a whole bottle of hairspray in it to make it stay there, and she was wearing a tight black dress, *very* short, that hugged her smooth curves.

I took another gulp of my wine as she linked her slender arm through mine and led me away from Chris. She pulled me into the kitchen and topped my nearly empty glass up. Then she walked me outside to the verandah, where a bunch of girls from school were glamourously spread over some cushions.

'Hey, Sylvie,' they said in unison.

What the hell? These girls know me? They aren't telling me to piss off? Hannah pulled me down onto the cushions. I drank and listened while they talked and laughed about boys and boys and mostly boys, and then one of them, Natalie with the big blue eyes, said, 'Are you going to sleep with Chris, Sylvie?'

I choked on my wine. They exchanged glances as I tried to recover, and Hannah helpfully whacked me on the back, causing me to spill more of it on my legs.

'Um. Am I supposed to?'

Another look exchanged.

'Well, maybe, y'know …' I trailed off, unsure of what I'd just walked into with that 'maybe'. Suddenly I felt sick.

The girls twittered like a flock of gossiping birds and carried on talking. I had nothing to contribute to the conversation and wouldn't have spoken up if I did, so I just sat and mindlessly gulped down what was left of my wine.

Truth was, I was already pretty drunk. Wine was

different to Baileys. I'd never had more than half a glass of wine before and that was always mixed with lemonade. 'Spritzers', Pamela called them. I was drinking too fast. The girls' voices and the music seemed to be coming from somewhere further off and the world was starting to feel more than a little off-kilter.

Maybe I was swaying. Some guy wandered over.

'You girls want a spliff?'

They did. The 'spliff' went round, each of them taking one puff and holding it for what seemed like a long time. The smell was pungent and permeated the air. It didn't help my queasiness. Someone offered it to me, but I shook my head.

'Hugs, not drugs,' I said and to my surprise, they just laughed. Where had that come from? What was going on? I didn't even know if I could stand up.

'Sylvie, do you know how to kiss?' asked a girl called Aria.

'Um, yeah, I guess …' *Well, that was convincing.*

'Cos, you don't want to disappoint Chris y'know.'

'What? Oh, yeah. I know.' My mind was foggy. My tongue felt fat and foreign. I knew they knew I was drunk.

'Well we'd better test you!' she crawled towards me with more speed than I could back away, and before I'd registered what was happening her lips were all over mine. I tried to push her away but I was so clumsy in my drunken state, and actually faintly curious, that I made no impact. I had never been kissed before, obviously, and Aria's lips were so soft. She tasted like onion dip mixed with wine and peppermint-flavoured lip balm. Just as I felt myself relaxing, she pulled away, eyes bright and face flushed.

'She's all right,' she laughed.

'Well that's good to know,' Chris's voice behind me was husky and slow, like he'd been yelling over the music and drowning in drink. He held out a hand.

'Come.'

I looked at the girls, who were all grinning. Hannah nudged my shoulder.

'Don't disappoint him,' she whispered.

The night air was so thick, I felt all hot, and all I could think about was how badly I wanted to dive into the ocean and swim away. *Is this what being popular means?* I put my hand reluctantly in his. He hauled me up and I stumbled into him. He steadied me with hands on my shoulders, and led me away.

Thirteen

I ran like there were ten rabid wolves snapping at my heels. The hungry darkness swallowed me up as I pushed against it. I didn't look back.

Blood pumped chaotically through my veins, jelly legs underneath me. Tears fell, dragging mascara down with them.

It was unsafe to be out at this time of the night by myself. I didn't care. The whole shitfaced world wasn't safe was it? I stumbled to a halt at the bus stop and waited for the midnight bus to come and take me away from my nightmare. I was Cinderella in tatters, and there was no prince to come and save me.

The bus rolled around the corner and pulled up with a screech of brakes and a slow puff of exhaust. I hauled myself up and avoided eye contact with the bus driver. He didn't look at me either. There were a few people already on the bus. A young couple with their faces all over each other, a group of giggling girls at the back and a boy slouched in a corner whose head kept dropping with the weight of his intoxication. They looked at me, and looked away. Indifferent. Did no one care? Would they have cared if I was their little sister? Would Cate have cared if she was here?

I took a seat and watched the lights of the suburb blur as the bus drove on. I felt empty. I pinched myself hard in the hopes that I was mid-nightmare. No such luck.

Because it was the late bus it didn't go as far and I had to swap buses in town and go through the whole ordeal all over again; sitting alone and small, on a bus with strangers who couldn't care less. When it got to my stop I threw myself off it and began the walk home.

It was the longest trip home of my entire life. I'd cried myself out and my feet were dragging under me. No car in the driveway meant no parents at home. Relief lifted some of the weight off my shoulders.

I let myself in.

The shower was steaming hot, hotter than I usually had it. I scrubbed and scrubbed and scrubbed my entire body until it was red, raw and sore. I let the sound of the shower drown out the sound of my sobs, gasping and choking on the water. I washed my hair three times. Finally I got out, thinking my parents would get home eventually and berate me for being up so late. I couldn't handle being yelled at.

In bed with the blankets pulled up over my head, curled into a small ball, I wanted to sleep. I wanted to forget, but I couldn't. Memories and feelings kept pushing through the surface of the fog in my mind, and I hid further under the blankets as if I was hiding from him.

He'd taken me upstairs to his room. I was drunk and my legs were wobbly. I hadn't totally grasped the whole situation until I was sitting on his bed and his breath was hot in my ear. He reeked and his clammy hands were all over me.

He asked if he could have some of what Aria had had, turning my face up to his and pushing his mouth on mine fervently, uncomfortably. His breath tasted like cigarette smoke mixed with alcohol and something like stale chips. His lips were chapped. No peppermint lip balm.

I gagged and tried to get away but he put his hands on my shoulders and pushed me backwards to make me lie down. He was leering as he lay down on top of me. The weight was crushing.

The room was spinning. I felt sick.

He was rough with my skirt, his hands snaking up my legs and yanking my knickers off. I tried to cry out but no sound came. I struggled to get out from under him but his weight and determination had me pinned there. He started fumbling with his jeans and I had to suffer him wriggling all over me trying to get them down. I knew what was going to happen. I just didn't know how to get out of it.

'Come on baby,' he breathed. 'Don't disappoint me. Or do you prefer the girls?'

No – I hated everyone – I hated myself – my breath was ragged – I couldn't wipe my tears – couldn't move – scream –

It burned.

I cried.

I *tried* to scream.

I said 'no, no, no' like a mantra, until he eventually put a big clammy hand over my mouth.

This was what I'd done to my life. There I was with a filthy, smelly, drunk boy on top of me, taking away any dignity I might have once had, with his hand over my mouth, pressed into my face, and tears running freely, soaking the pillow underneath my head. I had never felt so unloved and humiliated in my life as I stared at the light in the ceiling and waited for it to be over.

In the still silence of the night, I squeezed my eyes shut and heard the sound of the car entering the driveway. The lock rattled, and footsteps stopped briefly outside my room; they were most likely checking I'd turned off my light and gone to sleep.

I listened to the hushed tones of voices bidding each other goodnight and then separating. I understood now why they slept in different bedrooms. I never wanted to be close to anyone ever again. Eventually sleep took over but it was disturbed and I woke several times, sweating, gasping, feeling crushed.

At one point I remembered I hadn't checked for demons under my bed before I climbed in. Maybe I'd finally realised there were no demons under my bed.

They were inside me.

Fourteen

The following week was study leave, but the school was putting on revision classes for those who wanted to attend. I had planned to, but couldn't face it come Monday. Still pummelled with flashbacks of Saturday night, I was determined to put what happened aside, and I refused to be subjected to the taunting and gossip I knew would come if I showed my face at school.

I wanted to avoid everyone who had anything to do with school. I said goodbye to my mother in the mornings and then went to the city library, where I buried my nose in study. I would go to the exams. That was it.

How could the school get angry if I was still passing exams? I'd learn my textbooks inside out and back to front. I was making flashcards and posters and could nearly recite French off the top of my head. But I couldn't lift the feeling of sadness that hung like a shawl around my shoulders.

Je suis triste. I am sad.

Je suis mauvais. I am bad.

Je suis sans valeur. I am without worth.

I was getting texts from Belle. Why? Sometimes she would even call me. I never answered. I never replied. I wondered if maybe the rumour mill had started and people knew about what had happened with Chris. Every time I thought about him I felt like I needed a shower. Every night I woke up feeling the weight of him crushing me.

The minute Lorelei found out about it, it would be all over the school.

I was so afraid of what people would think.

What would Adam think?

Why should I care what Adam thinks?

He was one of them wasn't he? Just because he wasn't there on Saturday didn't mean he wasn't out screwing one of the other pretty girls from school. If I was being honest with myself, he was probably just like Chris. Would I have been this upset if it had happened with him instead of Chris? The answer, I knew, was yes.

Most days I stayed at the library until the evening, only going home in time for dinner and then shutting myself in my bedroom until morning. Late one afternoon I was packing up my books when I was startled by a voice.

'Sylvie?'

I turned around to face the uncertain owner. Belle stood before me, her beautifully magnified eyes blinking. Searching my face for some … recognition? Or maybe some sign that it was okay to speak to me.

'Hi.'

'Hi,' she replied, hugging her books to her chest. 'Have you been here the whole time?'

'Pretty much. This is where I hide most days. Studying, y'know.' *Hiding*.

She nodded slowly and pursed her lips. 'You haven't been at any of the revision sessions.'

'Yeah, well, I figure it's time best used in the library studying. Not much point in going to class so close to exams …' Probably one of the most ridiculous statements I've ever uttered. She didn't buy it. I could see it in her face.

'Let's get something to eat?'

Where has our friendship gone?

'Sounds good.' I whipped out my phone and sent a text to my mother.

Me: Having tea with Belle in town.

The reply was fast. The family matriarch was a speed texter, probably due to her nimble journalist fingers.

Pamela: Ok darling not home anyway.

I threw my phone back in my bag with disgust. Of course I'd expected it, but that didn't mean it didn't sting a little.

Belle and I walked side by side through the streets, towards our recently discovered favourite Mexican restaurant. It was cheap and authentic and decorated with the tackiest, brightest ornaments and strings of lights you've ever seen. But the food was the best ever. The streets were already beginning to get a Christmas feel to them. Some of the shops had decorations up in their windows and Christmas bunting over the entrances. The streetlights had ornaments attached high up and at the end of the street, the huge pine tree was lit up with lights. Normally I loved Christmas, but these days I didn't love anything. And it was only November, for crying out loud.

We wandered into Alimento Bueno and were shown to some rickety seats. After placing our orders with the cheery Mexican waiter, we both stared quietly at the table for a minute. Stealing a glance at Belle I saw that her lips were moving as if she had something to say, but wasn't sure if, or how, she should say it. Eventually, she looked up at me and blurted it out.

'Is it true you slept with Chris?'

There. That was it. It was out and there was nothing I could do about it. Belle leaned back in her chair, as if afraid of what I might do.

'Is that why you've been trying to track me down?' I asked hotly. 'You just wanted the latest gossip!'

Her mouth fell open. She looked genuinely taken aback that I would accuse of her of something so unBelle-like. I took a breath.

'You shouldn't believe everything you hear,' I said, calmer.

'So it's not true?' she said.

Yes, it's true, it's true, it's true ...

'So it is true.'

'I didn't want to.'

To my surprise, Belle put her hand on mine. Her face was filled with concern.

'I know that,' she said.

I stared straight into her big eyes.

'Really?'

''Course. You're not that kind of girl.'

Is anyone?

Grateful, I gave her a smile and she smiled back at me. Did that mean we were friends again? I hoped so. I really needed someone like Belle in my life. Her mouth was moving again but I knew it was going to be something helpful that I needed to hear.

'Did he use protection?'

Wait.

What?!

'Sorry?' I managed to spit out, pulling my hand out from under hers.

She sat back again abruptly, still wary of how I would react. Clearly struggling to find the right words to use as a damp cloth to ease the verbal face slap she'd just given me.

'I just meant: if you didn't want it to happen, was he safe?'

I imagined her horror if I told her no – he wasn't safe. I struggled to recall the details. It was a scene that replayed in my mind over and over, but it was more like flashes of memories, almost like a movie trailer. I hadn't been thinking about whether or not he'd used a condom – I'd just wanted it to be over.

'No, I don't think he used anything.'

Belle shifted in her seat and focused her eyes on the strung up lights. They looked like glitter reflected in her glasses. She was as uncomfortable as I felt. 'Did you, at any point say that you wanted to stop?' she asked.

My burrito was steaming hot and looking quite delicious. But suddenly I had no appetite.

'Yes.'

'But he didn't? Um – stop, I mean.'

'No.' This, from me, a whisper.

'That's rape, Sylvie,' she said.

Fifteen

It was 3am and I still couldn't sleep. I padded to the kitchen to make a Milo. As I waited for the kettle to boil I searched the pantry for the Milo tin only to find it empty. Sighing, I grabbed the vanilla essence and made a hot vanilla instead. Mostly milk, with a hint of vanilla and a splash of hot water.

When I was little my mother would do this for me if I had a nightmare. They'd both get up, and my father would make a big deal of checking my wardrobe for intruding ghosts, and my mother would sit on the bed and stroke my forehead until sleep stole me back. She was a pretty good mum when I needed her like that.

Now I needed her and she was lost to me. Someone I couldn't approach or confide in. Someone who never even told me she loved me. I couldn't remember the last time she'd told me that. Or even the last time she'd hugged me and told me things would be all right.

Calamity Cate was the Queen Bee of our house. A hug-hogger. I always felt she got hugged more than me. I also had a feeling that if anything happened to her, that would be the end of us as a family. No hugs again. I thought my parents knew that too.

I sat in my bed, surrounded by pillows and cushions and sipped my hot vanilla. I'd heard it said that if you can't sleep, it's because you're awake in someone else's dream. I wondered whose dream I was awake in. What was I doing? What was I wearing? Was it a dream, or was it a nightmare? Hopefully I was awake in Adam's dream. I wasn't over my world series crush on him, but I was avoiding him for ... *how long?* I didn't know. I was so afraid and ashamed that he might know about what happened with Chris.

My stomach turned as it dawned on me that I could be awake in Chris's dream. I pulled my blankets up further and wished with all my might that he would be hit by a truck. Or that Adam would beat him up and send him packing out of town and out of my life forever. For some reason, I thought if he was out of the picture I could forget the whole thing. Deep down I knew that wasn't so. I'd never forget. And I hated him for it. So much.

Belle's voice kept rolling around in my head: 'That's rape, Sylvie ...'

Was it? I hadn't thought about it that way. It didn't seem right to me. Rape was something that a stranger did to you. And you had to be kicking around and flailing your arms and screaming … Didn't you? *No, no, no* … Was that me?

Anxiety out of nowhere started playing with my heart, thumping it in its cavity like a speedball. I put a hand to my chest in an effort to slow it but my lungs were being squeezed so tight I couldn't breathe. Two questions were forcing their way to the front of my mind, no matter how hard I'd been trying to shove them back. The only way to get them out, I decided, was to write them out.

Opening my bedside drawer, I pulled out an old notebook I'd used for writing poetry when I was hoping to be creative. The poems were average. I'd never really had anything to write about before. I wrote my anxiety-inducing questions down and sat back, staring at them. In written form, they didn't look so threatening. They could've been anyone's thoughts. On paper, it was like I didn't own them anymore. If I left the paper lying on the street for the wind to carry it to a curious stranger, the words, the thoughts wouldn't be mine – I would have no ownership of them. My name wasn't on them. I would be anonymous.

My whole life had been spent wishing I was anything but anonymous and now here I was – probably one of the most talked-about girls in my year. But none of the talk was good. I looked down at the page and read the words in a whisper:

'Was I raped?'

'What if I'm pregnant?'

I looked around my room, as if expecting someone to answer me. It was still; the only sound the gentle, steady ticking of the clock. If I was pregnant, how many times would this clock have ticked between then and now? I started to panic. Every tick marked another second that a frickin' alien baby could be growing inside me. I had to get it out. I'd been feeling sick a lot lately …

Morning sickness? I couldn't have a baby!

By this time I was creeping across my room to get the laptop. A sharp intake of breath as I climbed back into bed and grazed my hip bones. They were still bruised. Balancing the laptop on my knees and blinking in the glaring light, I googled 'pregnancy symptoms'.

Nausea, check.

Fatigue, check.

Mood swings … um, I'm a teenager.

The best proof, *expecting.co.nz* informed me, was to do a pregnancy test. As *if* I could walk into a chemist and casually buy a pregnancy test! What was I going to do? I clicked on a side link which read 'unprotected sex' and read on.

> If you have sex without a condom, you place yourself at a high risk, not only of unplanned pregnancy, but also of sexually transmitted infections.

'Oh my God,' I said aloud, pushing the laptop away

as if it was infected and covering my face with my hands. 'What if I've got fucking chlamydia?!'

I flung myself off the bed and charged over to the clock with its teasing tick. Flipping it over in my hand I ripped out the battery and threw it on the floor.

'I'm not pregnant and I don't have the clap,' I told it defiantly.

Anxiety had moved in all its furniture and taken up permanent residence in my chest. I needed something to take my mind off it. I deleted my google history and with shaking hands, returned the laptop to its place on the desk. Back in bed, I took up my pen and paper again and began to write like it was the only day left of my life. When I was finished, I read over my work.

> *You have left a mark on my body*
> *and a stain in my memory.*
> *You may have even left a legacy,*
> *but I have nothing for you.*
> *You have taken from me*
> *what you wanted,*
> *but there is nothing of me left behind.*
> *Do you feel remorse?*
> *Do you feel sorry?*
> *Do you feel?*
> *I hope the dusty fragments*
> *of my insignificance*
> *mingle with my tears, creating glue*
> *that sticks to you.*

With my thoughts no longer inside me occupying my mind, I placed the notebook back in the drawer before settling down into my haven of blankets and pillows. Thankfully, I fell asleep straight away.

Sixteen

Walking home from my English exam I mulled over how I may have done. I'd felt like the entire room was staring at me when I walked in and showed my face at school for the first time since the incident. Not wanting to entertain any thoughts about babies, chlamydia or rape, I had shoved them right to the back of my mind in a file called 'too much to handle', and filled my head up on exam business, studying, classrooms, how to write a badass essay, calculations etc. If I ignored the other stuff, maybe it would just go away.

A shrill ring from the depths of my bag. Probably Belle to ask how I thought it had gone. I rummaged, but missed it. The number on the screen … my brain did a quick scan for some recognition, but no. It wasn't a number I knew.

I kept the phone in my hand, and continued to walk. A couple of minutes later, it was ringing again. Same number. I didn't usually pick up the phone if I didn't know who it was, but something nagged at me. *What if it's something to do with the exam?* I pressed the talk button.

'Hello?'

'Hi, is this Sylvie Rivers?'

'Yes.'

'Oh hi, Corinne from Family Planning here. Just confirming your appointment tomorrow.'

'… sorry?'

'Your appointment at Family Planning? 11:30am, do you know where to come?'

Stunned silence. I was staring straight ahead in horror, and yet not seeing a thing.

'Are you there?'

'Yes, um, yeah, I know where to go. Thanks.'

'See you at 11:30 then.'

The second the call ended I rang Belle of the Books. She picked up on the second ring.

'So how did that go? I think I –'

'Isobel. Did you make a Family Planning appointment for me?' In my mind I could almost see her reaction. I wondered if she could see mine. 'Well?'

'Sylvie, don't be mad. You need an appointment, and we all know you wouldn't have made one yourself.'

Tears stung my eyes, blurring the street before me.

'It's not something you can run away from.'

I didn't like feeling vulnerable. I didn't like my friend making me cry on the street. How could she? I hung up on her.

Storming into the house I hurled my bag away from me with such force that it hit the wine cupboard and all my books came tumbling out. Kneeling to pick them up, it dawned on me that I was alone in the house with a cupboard full of alcohol. Why had this never occurred to me before?

I pulled open the little wooden doors and looked at all the bottles of alcohol standing up straight in a little bunch, like pins at the end of a bowling lane. I selected one at the very back; my parents wouldn't miss it. Even though no one was home, I ran to my room and hid the bottle at the back of my wardrobe, inside a gumboot. Rubber flavoured wine. Delicious.

The landline rang. I made my way down the hall towards it. I hated the sound of ringing phones. They were so high pitched and urgent. Why couldn't they play nice music instead? I was sure most people only answered to shut them up. Which was exactly what I did.

'Is Pamela there please?'

'No, she's out. Can I take a message?'

A random moment of confused muffled voices, while the caller put his hand over the receiver to clarify something.

'Am I speaking with Sylvie?'

'Yup.'

'Oh, I've got Cate here. Are you happy to talk to her?'

My stomach sank, and I had to suppress a groan. This was the last thing I needed.

'You don't have to,' the guy said. 'I know it's a bit scary sometimes.'

Some part of me wanted to cry and tell this sympathetic dude everything. I wanted to ask him what I should do. Tell him that dealing with Cate was the last thing I wanted to face. But Belle was right. I couldn't run away from everything.

'No it's okay, I'll talk to her.'

'Sweet, I'll transfer you to the patient phone.'

My sister picked up on the first ring. 'Hey, sis, how's it going?'

I hadn't realised how much I'd missed her voice.

Before I had a chance to answer, she started speaking again: 'There's this really cute guy in the male wing his name is Braxton and I'm definitely in love with him and there's this new girl whose name I can't remember who's in the room next door to me and she cries and cries every night and ohmigod Sylv it's so annoying and it keeps me up all night …'

Pressured speech was the term for this ramble. I couldn't get a word in edgeways. When she talked like this she reminded me a bit of an auctioneer selling a house, or a commentator at the horse races that Dad watched sometimes on TV. Holding the phone to my ear, I returned to my room and retrieved the wine bottle while she talked. It was white wine, and after the first couple of sips, I didn't have to screw up my face anymore.

'Sylvia,' she was whispering urgently now. 'There's a little girl who comes into my room at night. She says I killed her.'

Calamity began to wail and sob hysterically, repeating 'it wasn't my fault' like a broken record. Behold Sylvie the Second, drinking from a bottle of wine, listening to my older sister getting herself into a state over a figment of her imagination: someone she believed she'd *killed for God's sake*.

Calamity continued to wail. There was nothing I could do.

I hung up the landline and picked up my cellphone to text the other person I'd hung up on that day. I couldn't run from it. I tapped three words into the phone and hit send.

Me: Come with me?

It took her about ten seconds to reply.

Belle: Of course.

. . . . .

. . . .

Seventeen

. . . .

The clinic was a quiet office with women calmly coming and going, or sitting in the waiting room, legs crossed, reading magazines while they waited for their names to be called. Butterflies were practising for the Olympic gymnastics team in my abdomen. Or was it a baby? I imagined a baby tapping my insides, asking me not to get rid of it, panicking. Calling me Mum. I wiped perspiration from my forehead and took some deep breaths. Belle nudged my shoulder.

'You okay?'

I didn't reply. My voice had retreated somewhere inside me.

'Sylvie Rivers?'

My breath escaped and even as I was aware of Belle getting to her feet, my own legs seemed to detach themselves from my body. She was pushing on my back, urging me upwards.

'Come on, Sylv.'

One last deep breath and I stood, legs wobbly, and followed the smiling woman who'd called my name to one of the consulting rooms.

It was a warm day but the room was cool, the window open, looking out across the harbour. The woman smiled at me and my mind released its grip on fear. She was probably in her 30s. I could make out some fine wrinkles around her eyes but her face was still soft and youthful. Thirty-two, I decided. She wore her jet black hair in a topknot high on her head, a blood red top and lipstick to match. She had a non-judgemental air about her. I surmised that this was essential to work in an area full of irresponsible mistakes.

'I'm Alannah and I'm one of the doctors here,' she said. She looked between the two of us. 'Which one of you is Sylvie?'

I put my hand up. 'Me. This is my friend Belle.'

'Nice to meet you both.'

Her smile was weirdly disarming. It made me feel like I could tell her anything. In my head Family Planning was all hellfire and brimstone, but Alannah made me feel immediately at ease. I decided I wanted to be just like her when I grew up.

'What can I help you with today, Sylvie?'

My voice came easier than I expected. It was a relief to be able to tell someone – an adult, who would know what to do.

'Well, um. I might be pregnant. And also, I'm scared I might have an STI.'

Alannah's face remained impassive, as if I'd just told her I'd been wrapping up Christmas presents that morning and had had a cup of tea. Which, by the way, I hadn't. I'd had a cup of wine.

'All right, when was the last time you had sex?'

Cringe alert. My body temperature skyrocketed, and I could feel the colour crimson flush through me. Alannah read my mind.

'You don't have to be embarrassed. I just need to know so I can help you.'

She poured me a cup of water, which I accepted gratefully. I sipped and felt the coolness slide down my throat, easing my fierce heat and slowing the jackhammer in my chest.

'Um. It was a couple of weeks ago now, I think.' I didn't think. I knew exactly when it happened.

Alannah nodded. 'And did you use contraception?'

I played with the fraying seam of my shirt. 'Nope.'

She started rattling around the room, opening cupboards and taking out equipment, including a silver device that looked like something out of an episode of *Grey's Anatomy*. She yanked the curtain around the bed and turned back to me.

'Have you ever had a smear test before?'

'No!' I replied, alarmed.

'It's how we check for STIs, and any abnormalities.

It doesn't hurt but it does seem pretty invasive, so you just need to try and relax. If you could just whip behind the curtain, take off the bottom half of your clothes and hop up on the bed.' She was all business.

I was stuck to the seat. Panicked, I glanced at Belle, pleading, as if she could do it for me. She elbowed me and grinned, before addressing Alannah.

'Does she get any jellybeans afterwards?'

Alannah stood at the basin washing her hands and laughed. 'Afraid not, but you can have some free condoms.'

Belle slumped her shoulders and looked at me glumly. 'It was worth a try. I'll buy you some cake.'

The ice had broken a little, but I was still a nervous wreck.

'Don't worry, you're not the first scared girl we've had in here,' Alannah said. 'Trust me. I've done this a billion times.'

I had no choice. I stepped behind the curtain.

When it was over, Belle and I sat in a café and tucked into a slice of black forest gateau approximately the size of my head.

'A celebration!' my friend proclaimed, raising her coffee mug to clink. I touched her porcelain to mine and breathed in the rich smell of my hot chocolate.

'I'm not out of the woods yet though,' I reminded her. 'I still have to get the smear test results.'

'But you're not *preggers!*' Belle enthused, tucking into the cake. 'STIs can be treated anyway, but pregnancy is a life sentence.' She swallowed before continuing.

'Do you think you'll do it?' Ganache smudged the corners of Belle's mouth.

I didn't have to ask what she meant. It'd been playing on my mind since the minute Alannah had brought it up. She'd been asking me if it was my boyfriend, if I needed contraception, and telling me about the morning-after pill etc, and the story just kind of came tumbling out of me. She put her hand on mine as I cried and cried, and when I was run dry she encouraged me to consider the option of pressing charges.

'Belle's right,' she said. 'What he did is a crime. You didn't deserve it, but what you do with it is up to you.' From her desk drawer she pulled out a pamphlet with the word 'rape' in glaringly large font on the front.

'Here's how to do it if that's what you decide to do.'

She stapled a business card for Rape Crisis to the pamphlet and handed it to me. I stuffed it in my bag and thanked her, the word etched on my mind.

It took my breath away, the idea that I had been the victim of sexual assault. *A victim*. That's what she'd called me.

No, I wasn't a victim. The word suggested I was innocent. I'd let Chris lead me up the stairs. I'd put in a huge effort to look 'hot.' I had gone to the party against my parents' wishes. The obvious question I suppose then was why? And the obvious answer I suppose was I wanted to make a point. I thought I was showing the world who I was and that I was in control … Showing who? My parents? My school mates? Adam Allegro? The first genuine wave of relief washed over me as I reminded myself that I was not pregnant with Adam's sleezy friend's child. Not that it mattered much. He'd find out the rest.

Meanwhile, I was sitting in a coffee shop, gratefully NOT pregnant next to my friend who was trying her best to catch the frayed ends of my thoughts and pull me back to earth. I smiled at her big, earnest eyes and felt such a rush of appreciation for her. I had never had a friend like Belle of the Books. No one had ever held my hand and helped me wade through troubled waters before. I had grown up thinking Calamity Cate would do that. But Cate was someone I didn't know now, and it scared me.

The gravity of the situation hit me all at once and I was a popped balloon: deflated, in a heap on the floor. I was glad I had Belle to pick me up. She put her arm around my shoulders and hauled me to my feet.

'Let's walk,' she said, steering me out of the shop before I made a dick of myself and lost my shit in the middle of the café .

We walked towards the bus. We'd survived exams, and now the streets were pulsing with the excitement of summer holidays. I took in the tinsel and lights adorning shop windows, and the signs for the up-coming Christmas parade. Truth be told, I was definitely staring a little too intently at one of the signs. I mean, I read it about six times over to try and avoid making eye contact with Belle and her giant spectacles. She cared that I was upset but she wasn't going to let it go. Her feet were moving quickly, trying to keep up with me as she hoisted her bag further up on her shoulder. I moved my eyes to the traffic lights and studied them as though I was from Jupiter and had never seen such a contraption.

'Uhhh ...' That was a Belle noise.

I steeled myself for the brunt of her latest question and chaotically ran over a brush-off reply in my head.

'Watch out ...'

This wasn't what I expected. My head snapped around.

'What?'

'You're about to walk into a rubbish bin!' Belle exclaimed, grabbing my arm and saving me for the billionth time.

Seriously, a box of chocolates for a thank you just wasn't going to cut it. I sputtered with laughter. Belle laughed along with me, and then ...

'So, are you going to press charges?'

Yeah ... That question wasn't getting any easier to hear ... It felt like a gunshot to the abdomen, or at least, what I thought a gunshot to the abdomen would feel like. I was bleeding confusion and fear into my abdominal cavity.

I had been feeling this way in my sleep too. In my

dreams, the blood seeped from me, ran down my legs, and turned my white shoes a scarlet red.

'God, Belle, I don't know! He'll get in so much trouble and everyone would hate me.'

'Won't you hate yourself if you don't?'

Damn her brain.

I was searching my reserves for an equally insightful reply, but all my thoughts shut down abruptly when I heard a chorus of familiar voices yelling my name across the street.

Eighteen

For a second I thought I'd misheard, until their voices rang out again. Chanting from across the street in their sing-song voices like children in a playground. Lore-liar, Hannah Ho-bag, Aria, Natalie and the rest all standing at the lights, waiting to cross over to where Belle and I were standing, our feet glued to the concrete; the remaining fragments of my self-esteem melting into the asphalt.

'*Sylvie the Slut!*'

Passersby on the street appeared not to hear. The foot traffic continued to be congested, shuffling along on the corporate pigeons' lunchbreak. I was vaguely aware of people stopping abruptly and moving around me as I blocked their path. I noticed a couple of faces glancing at me and quickly flicking their eyes away. Probably believing I was a slut, but more interested in the closest place to get a sandwich. I hoped.

The lights buzzed. The pack was crossing. Their eyes were snapping and glittering with spite and their smiles were twisted with contempt. In seconds they would be standing in front of my face. *What will they do to me?* I felt Belle's hand on my arm, pulling me through the crowd of suits, laughing teens and Christmas shoppers.

'Run!' She ordered and my legs obeyed.

I ran as fast as I could, dodging footpath trekkers, scooting down side streets, running from my demons, my fears, my shame. Tears burnt like acid in my eyes, my face was contorted, my mind loathing. I could hear them behind me, still chanting. Or was I imagining it? I cut through a carpark and stumbled to a stop.

'Shit,' I panted, bending over with my hands on my knees. My lungs were screaming at me, my breath coming in ragged gasps. Easing myself up, I checked my surroundings. No girls in sight. I'd lost them. My phone beeped. Belle.

> Belle: I lost you! Are you okay?
>
> Me: Will be – just a bit puffed lol.
> Gettin bus home.
>
> Belle: That was a dick move on their part.
> I'll get my bus too. Ring you later.
> Get home safe xx.

I couldn't even remember which bus Bookish Belle got.

It was all I could do to hold it together on my bus. My body ached and my heart hurt. I wanted to make myself as small as possible. Not one scrap of self worth left. I hated being alive if this was what living entailed. My elation over not being pregnant had faded.

I was a slut. I was labelled. I had a reputation. I wasn't invisible anymore and now I understood why they said 'be careful what you wish for'.

Holed up in my bedroom, curtains drawn, phone turned off, pulse thumping in my ears, I considered never leaving my room again. I didn't feel like facing the world when I couldn't trust my composure.

There was a knock on my door. Before I could tell them to go away, it opened. It took a lot of effort to open one eye, and when I did I beheld the parentals standing on the threshold. Their faces told me they were not happy.

'If you're going to tell me off can you –'

'Sylvia did you talk to Cate yesterday?'

What? 'She rang but you weren't here.'

'So you decided to talk to her instead.'

'Well they asked –'

'What did you say to her, Sylvia?'

'What? Nothing! I couldn't get a word in –'

'Well you upset her. A lot. You're not to talk to her without asking us.'

It felt like I was standing in the middle of a tornado. Fury took my breath away.

'She's my sister! You have no idea what it's been like for me to have a sister in a fucking psych unit not to mention parents who aren't even around … because you don't care about me at all do you, you just care about crazy Calamity Cate and maybe she's the way she is because of you! I'm pretty sure I'm such a failure because of the way you've raised me – you don't even care about me, you don't even know what I've been going through –'

'Don't you ever speak to your mother and me like that again!' Damn-it-all Dave roared. 'You have *no idea* how lucky you are!'

They retreated from my doorway and slammed the door shut.

'You have *no idea* what I've been through!' I screamed.

I couldn't see a thing. It was like a red veil had been pulled over my eyes. Blind fury. I picked up the glass on my bedside table and hurled it at the door, right where their stupid heads had been. It shattered, a thousand shiny stars falling to the floor. I heard the front door slam shut. Presumably going to see the other crazy daughter. I stalked to my wardrobe and pulled the bottle of wine from my gumboot. It was half empty post yesterday's phone call with Cate. I gulped it mindlessly. Urging it to act quickly and take away my misery.

I was staring at the broken glass on my floor. If I didn't clean it now I'd forget about it and cut my feet on it later. A thought dived into my mind and floated tantalisingly to the surface. I knelt and ran my hand over the fractured shards on the carpet. They bit into my skin like tiny teeth. I picked up the biggest piece.

With a dizzying breath, I drew the sharp edge across the skin on my arm.

Blood started seeping slowly out of the new pink rent in my skin. Braver, I pressed harder, and my skin split like the skin of a ripe nectarine, thick scarlet fluid erupting out of it like juice. I gasped as I watched the blood run smoothly downwards, following the contours, making a map.

Finally I'd figured out how to get some of my pain, some of my life, some of what made me *me* out of my body. I wasn't holding onto it anymore. I felt a weight lift.

Nineteen

I lay on the floor in my room in a dead straight line, examining the two dead straight cuts on my arm, wishing I was dead straight dead. The shards of glass lay around me, discarded weapons. Gingerly, I stood up, took the biggest and sharpest piece among them and hid it in my jewellery box. I didn't know if I would use it again. Distracted, fascinated, enlightened and yet terrified, I held the arm out. Vermilion roads travelled down it – blood that had seeped from the cuts, intersecting one another, paths to nowhere. *Is this the answer? Do I want it to be?*

I picked my way across the glass-encrusted carpet and left the confines of my bedroom in search of the brush and shovel, bringing my bottle of wine with me. I hadn't realised until I stood up how much of the stuff I'd had. I briefly lost my centre of gravity, bumping into the door frame before clambering into the hall. Rubbing my shoulder where it bore the brunt of the door, I made my way to the laundry muttering 'brush and shovel, brush and shovel' over and over, giggling at the absurd pickle I'd managed to get into.

On my way back I stopped in the bathroom. The mirror showed a scene straight out of a horror film. There I was, softly swaying, hair a tangled mess, a blood-covered arm. I took a step closer to the mirror, challenging my reflection.

'Sylvie the Slut,' I whispered.

'Sylvie the Slut,' louder this time.

'*Sylvie the Slut!*' Screaming now, I grabbed a handful of hair and yanked it tight between my fingers because it was the only way I could think of to immediately contain myself. My heart was beating fast as if with urgency, reminding me I was alive.

In my bedroom again, I swept up the remains of the glass and tipped it into the rubbish bin. I ran a bath. While it was filling up I ran water in the sink and washed the intersecting maps on my arm away. The skin was tender and the blood gave the water a reddish tint. The bath was full and I poured in some of my mother's expensive lavender aromatherapy stuff. On impulse, before I got undressed and climbed into the bath, I switched the light off. The idea of my body repulsed me. I didn't want to face it.

Submerged in the warm dark, I closed my eyes anyway. The tips of my toes only just reached the end of the bath and I wondered fuzzily if I could slide under and drown if I fell asleep. The darkness made me sleepy. I imagined I was in a different world, a butterfly in a chrysalis, untouched by gossip, unaffected by pain. Asleep in my safe haven ...

Lavender-flavoured water filled my mouth and ears. My eyes flew open and my arms flailed as I struggled to haul myself into a sitting position. I sat spitting out water and tipping it out of my ears. The world sounded distant, like I was inside a seashell.

'Jesus.' I said to myself, peering over the edge of the bath where puddles of water had splashed on the floor. 'Apparently drowning is not an option.'

I ventured into the lounge. The parents still weren't home. I checked the clock on the microwave. It was 6pm. I probably had the house to myself for a couple more hours then. My stomach grumbled, reminding me that there was nothing in it. The money was on the table. I dialled the number and placed my order – after several attempts at the voice recognition robot, I finally had success.

It would be a twenty minute wait. This time I wasn't walking to the village to get it. I'd asked for delivery, partly because I didn't trust my legs to get me there, but mostly because I didn't want to risk meeting Adam. I made a cup of tea, flopped on the couch and switched on the TV. The news was full of sad stories as usual. A man who accidentally shot his friend while on a hunting trip – *how do you mistake a human for a deer?* – a child abducted, suicide/homicide, a group of tourists killed in a car accident … My mind boggled sometimes at the tragedy in the world.

The doorbell rang and I jumped, spilling almost-cold tea down my arm. Wiping it off hastily and pulling my sleeves down, I approached the door in my pyjama shorts, hair still wet and tied back. Not a scrap of make-up. Murphy's law and I have never seen eye-to-eye, due to the fact that it seems to rule my life. And so I shouldn't have been surprised when I opened the door to find Adam holding my pizza with a look of shock on his face that probably reflected mine.

'Oh shit,' I spluttered and moved to shut the door in his gorgeous face.

'Sylvie!' he thrust his arm out, and I gave in pathetically, opening it wider.

I couldn't look at him. I still felt half drunk! He smiled. My legs were jelly.

'Getting it delivered this time eh?'

'Well yeah, I was already in my PJs so …'

He grinned and took in my appearance. I cringed under the appraisal.

'No war paint.'

'Nope.'

But battle scars. I wanted to pull my sleeves up. To show Adam my hurt and tell him to make it go away. But I couldn't. This was my war. Telling Adam would only push him from my doorstep, and all I really wanted right then was for him to stay right there.

'How come you're delivering? Do you have a car?'

'I've got a scooter. I don't normally do deliveries but one of the guys called in sick.'

'You've got a scooter? That's so cool! Um, would you like to come in?'

He shifted his weight from foot to foot.

That's a no if ever I saw one.

'Um, yeah, okay. Just quickly, though. The manager will be pissed if I'm not back soon.'

What?! Adam Allegro was entering my *house?!*

When he stepped over the threshold, I thought I would remember that beautiful moment for the rest of my life.

I led him to the kitchen. He took my pizza out of the bag and placed it on the bench.

'Nice place,' he said.

'Hm? Oh, thanks …' I said vaguely, torn between gazing at his hotness, and worrying that he must have been horrified by the state of my unmasked face and old pyjamas. It felt so intimate, him seeing me like this. All my etiquette had flown out the window and I had to grasp at strings to form a coherent sentence.

'Would you … maybe like a drink?'

He glanced at his watch. 'Uh, normally I'd say yes but I really have to go soon, sorry.'

'Oh no that's fine. I remember you said that before, actually. I've just got a really bad memory sometimes –' I cut myself off. *Stop babbling you spaz!*

'So, you went to Chris's party.' A statement, not a

question, and it hit me like a steamroller.

'Yeah. I did. I didn't stay that long though …'

He nodded.

'Why weren't you there?'

'Studying.'

'Studying?'

'Yeah, y'know, that thing you do when you want to pass exams.'

'Oh, right,' I meant to laugh but it came out as a kind of wheezing snort. 'I just thought, y'know … they're your friends and everything …'

He looked faintly puzzled. Holy Huckleberry, perplexed had never looked so good!

'Not good friends. More like just guys I hang out with at school sometimes. Chris is on my cricket team.'

'Oh.'

We stood facing each other for what felt like an eternity and a millisecond. Too long to be standing there awkwardly, but too soon to say goodbye. If he had heard, I hoped he didn't believe it. Either way, he didn't say anything, and he obviously didn't hate me since he was in my house with one hand resting on the bench and the thumb of the other running over his glorious bottom lip. He made his Pizza Palace uniform look like Prada.

And then I realised that maybe the fact that he'd heard was the reason he was in my house. Sylvie the Slut. Did he think I was easy? Did he expect something? Should I have led him to my bedroom instead of the kitchen?

Adam cleared his throat, and I realised I was staring.

His cellphone beeped in his pocket, making us both jump a mile.

'That'll be work. Better boost it.'

He picked up his bag and I snatched the money off the table, handing it to him and turning on my heel for the door. I yanked it open probably a little bit dramatically, like we were in a soap opera.

'Well, thanks for the pizza. See ya round!' *Waaaaay too cheery, dearie.*

He walked past me and I just about died as his scent rushed up my nose.

'Enjoy,' he said, winking at me.

He *winked* at me!

'I must have nine lives,' I muttered, as I watched him walk down the path.

Twenty

'**B**elle you sound like a broken record!'
I was trying to stop a meatball from escaping my Subway sandwich.

Belle sipped her Coke and pushed her glasses up her nose.

'Well I'm sorry, I just want to know what we're facing here.' She broke her cookie in two and put one half in front of me. 'I don't think you can run forever ...'

I gave up on the sandwich and picked up the cookie. Then I promptly put it down again.

'Wait a second. Did you just say what *we're* facing?'

She nodded casually.

'You don't think I'd let you go through the whole ordeal alone do you?'

I stared at her.

'Aw, Belle! What did I do to deserve a friend like you?'

She laughed and her eyes crinkled up.

'I don't know but you're clearly very lucky!'

'I am,' I agreed, ignoring her humour. 'And I don't know if I'll press charges. I think it would make everything worse.'

'Sylvie, how can things be worse? You can't let him get away with this. How many other girls has he done this to?'

I played with my straw.

'Are you saying I should?'

'I'm saying it would be the brave thing to do. But I can see how it's also the hardest ...' She trailed off. 'I don't know what you should do, Sylv. Whatever you decide, I'll help you.'

I tried to quell the nerves that gnawed at my insides as I considered properly for the first time pressing charges against Chris. Belle was right as usual. It was the brave thing to do. I needed to stand up for myself and any other girls that Chris had done the same thing to. But this way? This way seemed complicated. I didn't want to be hated. I wanted to feel empowered. I wanted to teach him a lesson. I wanted my self-esteem back. I wanted people to point and laugh at him. To humiliate him. To take away his power. I felt like pressing charges would backfire. I would be hated. I would be even more humiliated. What would Adam think? I remembered his thumb running over his lip the night before.

'What are you smiling at?'

Oops.

'Nothing.'

Belle wasn't easily fooled. 'No, no, no. Normal people do not smile when talking about laying rape charges. What is it?' She slurped the last of her Coke and put the cup down, watching me expectantly.

I wasn't going to get away with it. I took a deep breath, buried my face in my hands and groaned.

'I have a really inappropriate crush on Chris's friend,' I said.

'*What?!*' Belle squealed. 'Holy Moly, what a time to develop a crush on one of his pack!'

'Well, to be fair, when he came over last night he said they weren't good friends. Just kind of … school friends … They're on the same cricket team.'

Belle was practically having a stroke in the chair opposite me.

'When he *came over!* Sylvie! What else are you not telling me?'

'No, no it wasn't like that,' I tried to explain through laughter. 'He delivered my pizza. And he came inside. And I was wearing pyjamas and no make-up.'

'Good!' Belle sputtered. 'I'm glad he got to see the real you.'

'I don't know what to do though. He's probably disgusted by me. Or he'll expect something of me next time he delivers my pizza …'

Belle sat back, thoughtful.

'I guess there's a possibility. But there's also the possibility that he likes you for real ... Maybe you should give it some time and let all this Chris stuff get sorted out.'

Belle wins, I thought, as we pushed back our chairs and stepped out onto the busy street. Christmas shopping was the order of the day. We wandered through department stores all decked out with boughs of holly and bright Christmas trees and I grumbled about having to get presents for my family. I picked up a gift package made up of creams and lotions for Pamela Panic; a gimmicky tie and a bottle opener for Damn-it-all Dave. What to get for Calamity?

I wanted to get her something that said everything I couldn't. I wanted to get her something that said, *I'm sorry I haven't been to visit. I hate myself for it but seeing you is scary.* Something that communicated everything that had been happening for me recently, and miraculously gave her the ability to understand.

I wanted to give her the old Cate back. The well Cate. My big sister. But I wondered if that was more of a gift for her or for me. Wandering into a cute jewellery shop with Belle trailing behind, my eyes scanned the room before settling on a display of silver necklaces. I was drawn to a chain with a little silver heart pendant. A bluebird of happiness appeared to be flying through it.

'She loves bluebirds,' I said to myself.

'What?' Belle said.

'This is it. This is what I'm getting Cate.' I took it off the display and held it out to her.

Belle moved closer to examine the little bluebird.

'It's really beautiful, Sylvie.' She was standing close to me and her hair smelt like lavender. She raised her gaze to the sign above the counter and pointed. 'And look, three for the price of two!'

I navigated the shop looking for something for myself. I had to take advantage of a deal like that! I looked at countless pieces of jewellery but kept coming back to the same heart with the bluebird of happiness. Finally, I took it as a sign. I thought I needed some happiness too. And this way, Cate and I would share something. A reminder and maybe a way to communicate some of the things I wanted to say. Pleased with my decision, I took the two necklaces up to the counter. The girl behind the counter was wearing teal eyeliner and so many rings I was surprised she could lift her hands. She looked at me and grinned.

'You need to buy another piece if you want to take advantage of the three for two deal!' she squeaked, speaking so fast I imagined all her words tumbling out on top of each other. 'Do you want me to keep these here while you look around?'

I mentally smacked myself over the head. I'd spent so long deliberating over one necklace I'd forgotten what the deal actually was! How was I going to decide on another one? My eyes searched out Belle for advice. She was on the other side of the shop seemingly entranced by the necklace she was holding in her hands.

'Hold on a minute,' I said to the squeaky girl. Belle saw me coming and put the necklace back on the display.

'What was that?' I asked when I reached her.

'A really pretty necklace. I can't afford it though – I've spent all my money on Christmas shopping.' She looked at it one more time. 'Maybe I'll put it on my wish list.'

The necklace was a dainty chain with a tiny silver star on it. In the centre of the star was a 'diamond' – inverted commas definitely necessary! It was just so Belle. I giggled with glee and snatched it off the display, carrying it over to the counter. The only thing that slightly ruined the moment was having Belle at my side as I was paying, telling me over and over that I didn't need to get her anything. I took it off the counter before Squeaky could put it in the bag, and thrust it at Belle who stared at me with her giant hazel peepers.

'If I could buy you a bookshop I would,' I said, taking it out of her hands and turning her around to fasten it. 'But this is the best thank you I can afford.'

Squeaky was watching us with a flaky look which was suddenly replaced by something else. Her mouth dropped open.

'Wait – I know you … I know you! You're the girl

who slept with Chris, right? The one with the crazy sister?'

My mouth dropped open.

What did she just say?

Slept with Chris.

Crazy Sister.

I stared at the girl dumbly.

'And you are?'

Belle had transformed from meek maiden to dragon damsel. She was glaring at Squeaky, almost growling.

The girl shifted her weight uncomfortably.

'Uh, Cass. I go to your school …

'Well we don't know you, which means that you shouldn't know about our business!' Belle linked her arm through mine and led me out of the shop. 'And anyway it's not true!' she yelled over her shoulder. 'Don't believe everything you hear. Especially at high school!'

She'd done it again. *Our business.* I looked at my friend as we got mixed up in the busy shopping crowds on the street. Even though I felt hurt and humiliated, I couldn't wipe the amusement off my face. She glared at me. The huff hadn't all been puffed out of her yet.

'What?'

The little star was sitting pretty on her throat.

'The necklace suits you.' I said. 'And I didn't know you could be such a pit bull.'

Twenty-one

I stared at the words on the page. My hands trembled and a breeze ruffled the letter, so the words were tossed around in front of me. My lips were forming silent particles of words; my vocabulary stolen by the wind. Impatient, Belle snatched it from my grasp and adjusted her glasses to read better. Behind the frames, her large eyes widened. She looked like a cartoon character as she stared at me.

'Chlamydia,' she breathed.

Shame flooded me. Belle rubbed my arm and I jerked it away.

'Don't! I'm diseased,' I said.

'You can't catch it from touching someone's arm.' She studied the letter again, then 'Okay, so you just make an appointment, like they say.' She looked at me, her hair a mess in the wind. It was like she'd divined my thoughts. 'Do you want me to make it for you?'

Belle of the Books, beautiful Belle. Always there for me. I looked at my feet. I couldn't believe I had chlamydia! I was so angry. I felt like I should have already known – but my body was so foreign to me I had no idea when something wasn't right with it now. I hated Chris so much I felt like the hate would swallow me whole. I blinked the tears back. I would not cry. Not now.

'Yes please,' I said to Belle.

That night I couldn't sleep. How could I? I had CHLAMYDIA. The clap. A frickin' STI. It was what I'd feared when I'd first consulted Dr Google in the witching hours all those nights ago. I'd been so relieved I wasn't knocked up, I'd sort of forgotten about everything else. Belle had managed to wrangle me an appointment for the following day. I allowed myself a smile as I remembered her impersonating me on the phone to Family Planning. 'But I've been called back for a follow up! I've got chlamydia! Even as we speak my fertility is flying out the window …'

I'd left my laptop in the lounge. Rolling out of bed I crept down the hall and retrieved it. I could hear Damn-it-all Dave's snoring tumbling down the hall. The walls creaked and groaned, as though they were sick of listening to it too. I closed my door quietly and navigated the bombsite that was my room – stepping over piles of clothes and the polished-off bottle of wine.

The wind blustered through my open window, causing the curtains to rearrange things on the mantelpiece, reprimanding me for being awake when good girls should be asleep. The cuts on my arm felt stretched and irritated; skin so frustrated that its best attempts to heal were futile. I'd developed a kind of gross habit of picking and itching the scabs at night when nightmares woke me up. My recently re-dyed hair fell over my face – *why does red fade so fast?* – a shade reminiscent of blood. Maybe I wasn't a good girl at all.

I turned the laptop on. The blue light illuminated my face. I took a breath and logged onto Facebook; something I'd been avoiding since the 'incident'. I scrolled through the status updates from 'friends', none of whom had contacted me to see how I was doing. Lore-liar took up the majority of useless space on my feed.

> Went to the movies with my girls tonight.
> So excited for Christmas! Hoping I get the
> bracelet I asked for. Spent a beautiful day
> in the sun with Hannah and Aria today!
> This is the life.

'This is the life!' I squeaked, in imitation glee. My face wrinkled in disgust. Typical Lorelei, trying to put a PR spin on her Facebook page. I'd have put money on her ice cream melting on her top and her succumbing to a searing sunburn – *this is the life, my arse.*

How it actually happened, I am unsure. It was like I was possessed. I don't recall making any conscious decision – my fingers began working on the keyboard of their own accord. Before I knew it I'd created a new Facebook account using my second, unused email address. I had a pseudonym: Amelia Anderson (alliterative, but not unbelieveable) and I was searching for Lorelei. When I found her name, along with her profile selfie of her sitting on some beach in a little bikini, face caked in make-up, my hand hovered over the mouse pad. I didn't want to add her as a friend. She wouldn't add someone she didn't know, and I'd be at greater risk of blowing my cover. Instead, I clicked on 'message' and typed four words to my former friend.

> Amelia Anderson: Chris Kirby has chlamydia.

> Send.

My heart thudded. This was the wrong thing to do. I knew it was. But how else could I get revenge? By tomorrow, Lore-liar would have spread this throughout the school community. And for once, she'd be telling the truth. I returned the laptop to its rightful home on the desk and climbed back into bed. Still, I was unable to sleep. I switched my light back on, exasperated, and pulled my notebook and pen out of my bedside drawer.

Draped in my cloak
of invisibility

I wander
through people
blinded
by their own light
and I cry out
that my light is fading
flickering
into a feeble glow
only ever noticed
in error
still, my muted light
burns
and I wander
among you
wishing
you could save me
and wondering
if I'm really here
at all.

Closing the book, I drew my knees up closer and began picking at the scabs on my arm. Fresh blood sprang to the surface. A ruby red pearl. I wiped it away with my hand. It dried immediately on my palm and the foreign substance felt sticky, my skin taut, as if saying, 'Hey, I'm pretty sure that stuff's meant to be on the inside ...'

I caught the metallic tang of it as I pushed my hair back and wondered how much blood I would have to lose before anyone noticed. I flicked my light back off, and sleep finally snatched me away.

Twenty-two

My phone was buzzing. Bleary-eyed, I stuck my hand out from under the covers and blindly reached for it, knocking bits and pieces from the top of the bedside table. Squinting and blinking, I held the phone up to my face to read the message more clearly.

Belle: Sylvia. Check Facebook. Now.

Like a speeding train it hit me: social media in the dark. *What have I done?* In the face of a new day, it seemed like a really really bad idea. Anxiety started hammering its family photos to the walls of my ribcage. Reminding me it was here to stay. I threw the covers off and raced into the lounge. It was Friday. No parents. I balanced the laptop on my legs, stuck straight out in front of me on the couch. Panic mounting, I logged onto Facebook.

> Um, who is Amelia Anderson and why
> is she telling me that Chris Kirby has
> chlamydia?? Is this true, Chris?

Lorelei was, as I had expected, all over it, and going straight to the source while letting the rest of the world know as well. I could see a career for her in a tabloid magazine.

My heart shifted from its fast tempo to a dull boom. She'd tagged me in her status. What if I was found out? I read through the comments on Lore-liar's revelation. There weren't as many as I had expected. I had expected laughter and jibes coming from Club Popular, but most of the taunts were from randoms at school. Nothing from his pack of girls, Hannah Ho-bag, Aria with the soft lips, Natalie of the big, blue eyes and co. Nothing. And then,

> Chris Kirby: The clap? Lol thts hilarious. I
> dnt even knw ne Amelia Anderson.

> Lorelei Ashton: Lol are you sure
> Christopher? You don't really remember
> all their names do you? :)

> Chris Kirby: Lol ur funny. Gve me sum
> credit!

First of all, I hate people who use outdated text abbreviations online. Second, I had a flat feeling my plan had failed. Defeated, I logged into my Amelia account. My mouth dropped open. I had three messages. One was from Natalie. The other two were from girls at school that I'd seen around but never spoken to. Each one said much the same thing:

> How do you know Chris has chlamydia?
> And why don't I know you?

Natalie asked the obvious question:

> Is this a fake account?
> Are you joking?

I replied to them all the same way:

> My name obviously isn't Amelia Anderson
> and it's a fake account because I don't
> want Chris to find out it's me. I go to a
> different school and met him at a party.
> One thing led to another and I ended up
> with the clap.

> No joke. Get checked.

Satisfied, I logged off. While all this was happening, Belle had been sending me a barrage of texts telling me to wake up and get on the internet and text her back.

> Belle: Oh no. What have you done?

> Me: Don't know what you mean? Let's
> have coffee after my FPA appointment.

> Belle: Ok and then you can tell me all
> about (how you became) Amelia Anderson.

Oh crap.

Alannah's office was all tinselled up for Christmas, which by now was only a week away. She twisted slightly on her spinning chair as she typed words into the computer. I studied her feet because I was way too embarrassed to look at her face. She had cute flats on.

'I like your shoes,' I murmured. 'I think if I worked here I'd wear heels though.'

She glanced down at her feet and then raised a perfectly shaped eyebrow.

'Until you realised how much you have to stand up in this job. Try doing an accurate smear test when you're having to shift your weight the whole time.'

I snorted. Elegant, I know.

'Shifting weight sounds good. Where can I shift mine to?'

Alannah eyed me carefully. She had fuschia lipstick on.

'What else is going on for you, Sylvie?'

Blindsided by the question, I didn't have an answer at the ready.

'What do you mean?'

She leaned back in her chair.

'I mean, being raped is a horrible thing to go through, and I'm wondering if you have anything else in your life that's going a bit wrong at the moment.' She paused. 'Did you decide to press charges?'

I was so over hearing that stupid question.

'Nope.'

Alannah nodded slowly, fuschia lips pursed. I wondered if she would've pressed charges if it had happened to her.

'I'd really encourage it, Sylvie. For one thing you're underage, and who knows how many other girls he's done this to. You wouldn't have to go through it alone.'

Bet she wouldn't have the guts.

'Yup.'

'Did I glimpse the edge of a bandaid under your sleeve before?'

I automatically tugged my sleeves down to my thumbs. 'Maybe.'

'Have you been self-harming?'

'Maybe.'

'Can I have a look?'

She reached for my arm and I gave it to her, letting her push my sleeve up and ease off the bandaids. I tried not to look at them. The two lines looked messy and gross, thanks to my scab-picking habit.

'They're not infected, but you need to keep them clean and stop picking them. Look for some healthier ways of coping with your hurt, Sylvie. Cutting is a nasty cycle. You'll regret it one day.'

She handed me a couple of clean bandaids and sat back in her chair.

'Is there anything else that's making you feel like doing that?'

I looked at her shoes again. They were pastel yellow with lilac lace over the top. The left one was slightly worn at the toe.

'No.'

'Do your parents know what's going on for you?'

'My parents don't know anything about me,' I said. I could almost taste the acid on my tongue. And before I could stop myself, 'They're too busy worrying about Cate.'

'Who's Cate?'

Alannah was leaning forward now, ready to listen to my story. My story. Not Cate's. And maybe it was the concern in her face, or the empathy in her voice, or maybe it was just the fact that she could see me and hear what I was saying, but in that moment my heart broke. Before I could stop them, tears were spilling out of my eyes, and I was telling Alannah that Cate was my crazy sister and no one cared about me because I was invisible. She held my hand and gave me tissues and made sympathetic noises and by the time I'd got my shit together, she'd handed me a card for a youth counselling clinic and told me she was going to make a referral.

'It's free. Your parents don't have to know.' She said, kindly. She handed me a prescription for antibiotics to kill off the clap and I stood up, puffy-eyed and drained.

'Give the prescription to the front desk. And make sure when the counsellor rings you, you make an appointment and attend. You're not invisible, Sylvie. You just need to learn to communicate your distress.'

Belle was waiting for me at a café down the road, and I ordered an iced chocolate before sitting down. She was looking at me gravely.

'Hi, Amelia. How was your appointment?'

I sighed and leaned in closer, looking around

conspiratorially.

'I got medication, bawled my eyes out and now I have to go to a frickin' counsellor. And how did you know it was me?'

Belle rolled her eyes.

'Who else would it have been? I looked at the profile when Lorelei tagged you and saw you had no friends, no pictures, no information ... and then there's the alliteration.'

I cringed. How had I not realised that Belle would see right through me? I hoped like mad that no one else would. My iced chocolate appeared on the table before me and I took a long sip before owning up. Belle waited, sipping her tea.

'I thought it was a good idea at three o'clock this morning all right? And as a matter of fact, I've got three messages already asking me how I know. I told them to get checked.'

'Oh my gosh, who?!' Belle's interest overrode her disapproval and her eyes widened to saucers as I listed each girl. Her face quickly darkened again.

'What if they find out it's you, though? What if Chris finds out?'

Fear rolled through my body. I hadn't thought this through at all had I?

'They won't.' I said with confidence. But anxiety was knocking on the door again, and I busied myself sipping my iced chocolate, which was as icy as my insides.

Twenty-three

Day five on clap-killing antibiotics and I felt like they were killing my soul as well. I had a metallic taste in my mouth which would not go away no matter what I tried, I had an upset tummy and, to top it off, not knowing or caring what the term 'photosensitive' meant, I'd sat out in the sun reading my book and my skin now matched my red hair. FYI: *sunburn*.

So I did what any self-respecting teenager would do. I hid in my room for days, only coming out for the odd meal when the parentals were actually present.

I spent a lot of time on the internet, checking my Facebook pages to see if anyone had said anything further about my revelation. I was more nervous than I cared to admit about people figuring out that it was me. I seriously considered changing my appearance yet again and switching schools the following year. I'd been so desperate to be noticed that I hadn't cared what form the attention came in. Now I did.

Christmas was only a couple of days away and I lay on my bed, my scarlet skin slowly fading, and daydreamed about how my favourite day of the year would go. Finally, *finally* I was allowed to see Cate! I would go with my parents to the hospital and we would bring breakfast and presents and spend the day with her. She wasn't well enough for leave yet – according to Pamela, the doctors suspected her of spitting out her medications, and she continued to have delusions and unpredictable freak-outs.

'Doesn't help that they keep dabbling with her medications,' Pamela said. 'She's rapid cycling as it is! You'd think they'd have got it right by now.'

I imagined how happy my sister would be to see me, and I could fill her in on exams and make up fun stories about what I'd been doing. *As if I could tell her the truth!* I would give her the necklace I bought her and show her my matching one. She'd love them.

Feeling motivated and brighter than I had in a long time, I ventured out of my room and followed my nose to the kitchen where I found my mother taking a tray of chocolate biscuits out of the oven. She was wearing an apron over her dress – old-fashioned but so 'Pamela' – and had slippers on her feet. Her hair was caught up in a scarf with strands falling out in places. She looked so … motherly.

She put the tray on top of the stove, took her oven mitts off and wiped her forehead with a wrist. Her face was flushed from the heat of the oven. Looking up, Mum saw me standing in the doorway. Her eyes were bright. This was her favourite time of year too.

'Sylvie!' she said, like she was actually pleased to see me. 'I'm just making some food to take to Cate on Christmas Day. I'm about to make the Christmas cake. Have a biscuit.' She gestured towards the tray on the stovetop. 'Careful though, they'll be hot.' She turned back to her work, and began sifting ingredients into a mixing bowl.

'Thanks,' I replied, taking a piping hot biscuit and trying not to gasp – shifting it from hand to hand and eventually breaking a bit off to put in my mouth. It burnt my tongue but was delicious.

'Yum,' I said, tentatively, and then, 'do you want some help?'

Mum turned and looked at me for a moment. She had a soft expression on her face. 'I'd love some help. First, you'd better put some Christmas music on!'

I went to the music collection and began flicking through it until I located the Christmas album I wanted. This was how we always did Christmas – baking and music. I'd missed the seasonal spirit so far this year. I'd put the tree up after exams had finished but it barely got mentioned. Now it looked like the spirit of Christmas had finally reinstated itself in our house.

We didn't say much during the baking, probably because neither of us knew where to start. I didn't mind. I was happy. Mostly we sang along and even had a dance-off in the kitchen. My Mother danced like such an idiot. While I was measuring out the flour she bumped my elbow, just like old times, causing me to cover myself in flour and dissolve into giggles. It was exactly what I needed.

Then she handed me the bowl. 'Make a wish.'

This was one of my favourite traditions. I took the bowl from her, closed my eyes and stirred. *I wish for happiness.*

Twenty-four

I'd spent the day wrapping presents, dancing to Christmas music and eating. *I'll go on a diet after Christmas.* Now it was late afternoon and muggy. I caught the bus to the beach, swimming togs underneath my clothes, all set for a swim. The sea was calling me. I wondered if Cate missed it. I was slathered in SPF 30 sunblock; although, thankfully it was my last day on antibiotics. Stepping off the bus, I inhaled the salty air and let the slight breeze cool my face.

What a perfect way to end the day. I found a spot on the beach, stripped off, and ran into the water with abandon. It lifted my feet off its sandy surface and carried me as though I was weightless, raising goosebumps on my skin.

Vaguely, I became aware of a small voice to my right. Eyes closed, my forehead crinkled. Adrenaline started creeping through my body. I lifted my head slightly so the water wasn't in my ears. Listening.

'Help!'

Upright in the waves now, my eyes scanned the water for the owner of the voice. I could hear someone screaming on the shore. I looked and saw a small crowd of people with a woman at the centre, screaming, screaming. I put my arm up and to my right, pointing to the general direction I thought the 'help' had come from.

'Some direction please?' I muttered.

A couple of hands pointed and nodded. *Yes, over there*. I took a breath and submerged myself in the water. My eyes stung when I opened them and bits of seaweed drifted past as I swam, searching. It didn't take long.

He was young, probably around eight, and drifting down towards the seabed, his skin white and hair softly floating around his face. Later, I would think that I'd never forget that image – ethereal and alarming, peaceful and chilling all at once, but in the moment there was no time to think. I had to move. Fast. I powered through the water, grabbed the boy around the waist and kicked us up toward the surface. His dead weight in my arms was dragging me, but I fought as hard as I could with his little body slack against mine. *He's dead.*

Suddenly two lifeguards were next to me. 'Thanks, we can take him. Are you okay?'

I let them take the boy from me and my arms felt weak. I nodded numbly.

'You did good,' one of them said.

The woman's cries were getting louder as my heavy limbs took me closer to shore. The lifeguards were already on the beach working on the boy, surrounded by people gaping at the scene. No one noticed when I washed up on the sand. They were doing CPR, the mother was in a heap on the ground sobbing, and two other little kids – a boy and a girl – were being comforted by an adult. The boy was howling, face red, mouth wide open, and the girl was staring ahead at something. Staring … at me?

A warm trickle ran down my arm, amongst the cool droplets of sea water. The scab from one of my cuts had reopened. Blood oozed out of it and I wiped it away, smearing it on my skin. The little girl was watching.

I was a monster.

Tearing myself away from the group, I picked up my clothes, and ran to the public toilets. I could still hear the woman's screams and the boy's howling behind me.

I slammed the cubicle door, dried off and pulled my clothes on. Breathless and shivering, I sank down on the toilet seat, trying to conjure the sound of crashing waves to take my mind off it. Once I'd collected myself I snuck out and ran to the bus stop. The bus was pulling up. So was the ambulance. I launched myself onto the bus and into a seat. Shock and shame washed over me again and again like a wave.

Twenty-five

I was clearing the dinner table later that night when it was on the news.

A nine-year-old boy almost drowned at Darling Bay this afternoon, but for the heroic actions of a mystery teenage girl. The girl was swimming when distressed relatives of Daniel Reed's noticed he had fallen off his boogie board. Daniel was rescued and carried halfway to shore by the teenager where lifeguards and paramedics were able to revive him. He is to spend the night in hospital for observation. The young heroine disappeared before anyone could thank her.

The camera showed a picture of the beach and then cut to a shot of the boy and his mother in the hospital. *He's alive!* 'Whoever that young woman was,' the mother said through tears, 'I want to thank her from the bottom of my heart for saving my boy.'

'Sylvia?' Dave broke through my reverie.

I was frozen, a pile of plates in my hands, a lump the size of the Hope Diamond in my throat. I had saved a life. There was a boy sitting in a hospital bed, alive and loved, because of me. And all I'd cared about were my stupid wounds.

'Sylvia?'

'What, Dad?' I looked at him sitting in his armchair, staring at me like I was from another planet. *Should I say?* I wanted to tell him about my triumph. My success. They'd called me a heroine! He'd be so proud. *Wouldn't he?*

'Everything okay? You seem distracted.'

'Yeah, I'm fine.'

'I think I'm getting used to that red hair of yours. Or is it pink?'

I groaned. 'Da-ad, it's red. It's just fading again.'

He nodded and turned back to the TV. 'Sometimes you look just like your nana, you know.'

'Nana has white hair, Dad.'

'She *had* red hair. Back in the Jurassic period. I'll have to get out the pictures and show you one day.'

'That would be cool.'

The six o'clock news continued in the background. A lady was talking to some old man about the weather. We were having an incredibly summery summer – one of the hottest on record, and the humidity was out of this world.

I made a coffee for Dad, and tea for Mum and me. I was putting them on the coffee table, when Mum came in and took up her place on the sofa with a blanket and her book.

'Thanks, love,' she said, and looked at me over the top of her reading glasses. 'Are you coming with your father and me to church tonight? You're the only one who knows all the words to the Christmas Carols. And your father will fall asleep.'

'I don't sleep in church!' Dad was all mock indignation. 'We only go once a year. I'm catching up on my prayers. They don't work if you don't have your eyes shut.'

I giggled. 'Yeah, okay.'

Feeling slightly giddy with a combination of pre-Christmas Day excitement, love of midnight Mass, and the all consuming, sticky heat, I rolled on the balls of my feet and my eyes flicked curiously around the church. Orders of service were being used as makeshift fans, and sweat was being wiped from brows in every direction I looked. I thought the choir people might expire at any second with their heavy white outfits, standing so still in a cluster. I saw no one I knew.

After the Christmas carols was the actual service. I didn't know the majority of the songs and felt self-conscious bowing my head in prayer. I wasn't even sure what I believed. I observed the other overheated people taking up the pews. Every one of them had a story and probably a few regrets. Just like me. And here they all were, *standing with me.*

Right at that moment, in the hot, people-filled church, that was all I needed.

At the end of the service, as we were filing out into the night, a cooling rain began to fall.

Twenty-six

When I awoke on Christmas Day the rain that had sent me to sleep like a lullaby had ceased, and in its place a brilliant blue day was forming. I grinned and stretched like a cat in my bed before throwing the sheets off and swinging my feet to the floor. I could hear my parents' movements in the kitchen and padded down in my slippers to wish them Merry Christmas. The sound of carols dribbled down the hall as I approached.

In the doorway I stopped abruptly. I actually had to blink a couple of times to check my eyes weren't deceiving me. My mother and my father locked in embrace. *KISSING! What the* …? This never happened. Like … ever.

Stunned but fizzing with happiness, I backed up a couple of metres and commenced my walk to the kitchen again – this time making sure my footsteps were heard.

They had recovered themselves. Mum was busying herself packing a chilly bin with salads and desserts and other such edibles that made my mouth water. Dad was putting presents into a box. My mum smiled at me, a heartbreakingly happy smile, and even Dad's face seemed more relaxed.

'Merry Christmas, sweetheart,' Mum said, giving me a peck on the cheek and the smell of her perfume was at once familiar and distant in unison. A scent from my childhood.

'Merry Christmas,' Dad said gruffly. 'No presents yet. We're waiting until we see Catie.'

'Yup. Merry Christmas to you too. Do you need help with anything?'

'Just have a shower and be ready in twenty minutes, love,' my mother turned back to her chilly bin. I scooted down the hall and had a shower in record time. I chose a black dress with white polka dots and red and black stripey socks that reached my knee, but I spent the majority of the twenty-minute time limit attempting to gain control of my hair and putting on thick black eyeliner. I stood back and appraised the finished product. Still chubby, but I would do. I was almost exploding with the excitement of seeing my sister. I hoped she'd like the makeover.

We parked across the road from the hospital since the general consensus was that the hospital carpark would be chock-full of other visiting vehicles. Our spot was under a tree overlooking a park and, beyond that, my beautiful sea. I hoped that Cate could see it from her window.

Seagulls loitered, some briefly touching down before taking off again, and others hanging around waiting for any food the picnickers might donate. Sparrows flitted back and forth, tilting their heads with an air of inquisitiveness, and puffing out their little chests with false bravado. Children played in the playground, testing out their new presents while their adults looked on.

A little boy sent a Frisbee spinning through the air and his cute Jack Russell leapt up and caught it in his mouth.

The thick, humid air pulled sweat out of my skin the second I stepped out of the car. I wished I could wear short sleeves. A guy whizzed past me, and I jumped out of the way. The music coming out of his headphones was louder than the wheels on his skateboard. A girl sat with her back against a tree, reading. She looked like she was having a picnic for one. No – for two. I watched as a guy crept up on her with flowers behind his back. She laughed and kissed him. I thought of Adam, and wondered what he was doing for Christmas.

'You might get a shock, Sylvie,' Dad cautioned me as we crossed the street with our armloads of food and presents. 'She's not responding too well to treatment this time around. Not sure if she's taking her meds –'

'Of course she's taking them!' said Mum. 'She's a good girl and surrounded by nurses all day. Surely someone would've seen by now if she was spitting them out.'

'Oh I'm sure they've got a handle on things, Pam. But she's not always easy to manage as you well know. And she managed to spit her pills out in a nurse's face the other week …'

A laugh escaped me before I could stop it. Both parents looked at me with raised eyebrows. 'That's so Cate,' I sputtered, wiping perspiration from my face and hoping I didn't now resemble a panda.

My mother bristled a little and continued to stride purposefully into the hospital, eyes straight ahead, determined to have a good day. My father, to my surprise, remained in step with me, and gave me the shadow of a rare smile and a discreet wink. I beamed back at him.

Mum stepped up to reception and rang the bell. While we waited for someone to come, another family walked in behind us. A young woman with a kid who looked around three, and a baby balanced on her hip. She smiled at us briefly before the baby dropped its dummy at her feet. I bent and picked it up, offering it to the baby, who took it with wide eyes, dribble all around its mouth, and then shyly flicked its head away, looking over the woman's shoulder.

'Thanks,' the woman said and hoisted the kid

further up on her hip.

The older one, a little girl, was clinging to the huge bag the woman was holding, her other hand holding a brand-new Barbie. She saw me looking at her and thrust her arm out to display her toy for me.

'I got a Barbie for Christmas!' she crowed.

My parents smiled and murmured phrases along the lines of 'aren't you lucky'. I studied the plastic doll in her hand. It looked like a stripper. The woman put her bag down and entered into some dialogue with my parents about how her sister was a patient – *mine too* – and how she had been visiting her every weekend since she was admitted, which actually wasn't too long ago.

A lady came bustling down the hall, and after determining who we were there to see, buzzed us in through the main doors. My dad had picked up the woman's giant bag, which he juggled valiantly with the box full of Rivers' family presents, and she walked in ahead of us. Her sister met her at the door and threw her arms around her, kissing her on the cheek and wishing her Merry Christmas before picking up the little girl and making a fuss of the baby. I watched with excitement. Was this how Cate would greet me? I hadn't seen her in so long.

A pang of guilt hit as we were ushered into a visitors' room, and the things we had brought were sifted through by the woman who had let us in. Once satisfied, she announced that she would check out the presents for Cate once she had opened them. *Seriously?* We were family! As if we were going to bring in illegal drugs or a gun or something. The woman made to leave.

'I'll go and get Cate for you,' she told us. 'Just be aware she isn't having a good day so far.'

We sat in nervous silence and I fidgeted with the rings on my fingers as I awaited the sisterly reunion.

Twenty-seven

We heard her before we saw her. Her feet thumping down the hall, and her voice, so familiar, getting louder with each step. Something was wrong. Pamela Panic's eyes flashed at Damn-it-all Dave's, the panic flares emanating from them both. Cate's words didn't make sense to me. They didn't fit with the happy script I'd been coming up with in my head. I had a feeling I wasn't going to get the greeting I'd hoped for. I braced myself in my chair and tried to make myself as small as possible.

And then she was there.

My big sis, Cate.

My heart felt stuck in this confusing jumble of feelings: swelling up with love and deflating with disappointment. She stood on the threshold of the visitors' room with bare feet, in a hospital gown. Her hair wasn't as golden as I remembered, and at some point she must have cut it off. It sat in a tangled, roughly cut bob around her face. She reminded me of a child, standing there with her birds-nest head of hair, wide eyes, shapeless gown and small naked feet. Her hands were balled in fists at her sides and she was breathing heavily. I remembered this posturing from times past. She looked like she was ready to attack.

And then her mouth opened.

Her mouth opened and her words were a torrent.

Her mouth opened and she was a hurricane.

Her energy burst forth and rolled around the room, leaving us speechless and unable to shelter from her fury. She was babbling almost in her own language and I couldn't keep up. My mother was crying and offering beseeching words.

'Calm down, honey, we brought you presents ...'

My father's head was cradled in one hand as he sat back in his chair. Defeated, frustrated. Staff members were involved now, trying to talk Cate down – but she was having none of it.

And then her eyes found me.

There was no recognition in them at all. Zero.

She stared for what seemed an age.

I opened my mouth, uncertain.

'Cate?'

She snapped back to life and lunged at me. I had nowhere to go. The two staff members grabbed her arms and hauled her bodily from the room. She was shrieking like something out of *The Exorcist* and what she was saying turned my blood to ice.

'Who are you?!' she screamed. 'Who the fuck are you?! Where's my sister?!'

My parents were standing, looking at each other and then at me. Then my mother was wiping her eyes with a tissue, bereft of words and shoulders shaking.

Dad cleared his throat. 'Maybe you should go wait in the car, Sylv. We'll be out shortly.'

I stood shakily, and took the car keys from him. As quietly as possible, I stepped into the hall. My sister was lying on the floor on her stomach, her arms pinned on each side by the two staff members who'd rescued me. More staff were just arriving. Quiet as a mouse, I crept down the hall and pressed the button to open the doors. Once they closed behind me, I stopped and peered through the small window.

They were helping her up, one on each arm. She was quiet – a ragdoll between them. Her head hung forward, and she looked as though she was asleep; as though the storm had passed; as though she was suspended in a dream. I had a disconcerting feeling that I wasn't present in my own body and was reminded of her words so long ago.

What if I'm dreaming now, and you're not real?

I wrapped my arms around me to stop myself falling apart, and walked as fast as my legs could carry me out of the building, across the road to the car, where I fell into the backseat and cried. Wailing, snotty, ugly tears … I cried until I couldn't distinguish between my tears and beads of sweat that were seeping from my skin from the pent-up heat of the car. Over and over and over again the thought clanged like an alarm in my mind: *you're even invisible to your sister.*

Then, maybe because it was Christmas Day, or maybe because people really are kind, two things happened.

The first thing I noticed was a family getting out of the car next to ours. It was a mum and a dad and three kids. Two of the kids looked the same age and very similar. Twins? The other was a toddler still sitting in his car seat. While the parents grappled with getting him out of his seat and unloading picnic baskets and assorted items, one of the girls was busy trying to get the dog to obey her orders, index finger out, stern look, mouth forming the word 'sit', and her twin held what appeared to be a colouring book.

This girl noticed me sitting in the car snivelling and looking highly glamorous (note the sarcasm), and blinked her big dark eyes under her mop of shiny dark hair. She stared at me gravely for a second, looked at her parents to see if they had noticed this mess and then seemed to make a decision. She opened her book and leaned it against the window of our car, the window I was looking through. She appeared to be writing something.

The cover of her book, pressed against the glass read *Fairies of the Meadow* and was decorated with whimsical depictions of fairies set against a pink background. It would've been right up my alley when I was eight and became convinced I was in fact a house-dwelling fairy. Thinking she'd lost interest in me, I wiped my nose and looked away.

Seconds later there was a small thump on the window and I looked back to find the book now facing the other way, the inside cover pressed against the glass, and the words 'don't cry' written in childish scrawl with a smiley face drawn under it.

I laughed and wiped my eyes.

'You're lovely,' I said aloud, and she peered into my window from around the edge of the page to check I was reading it. I smiled and nodded. 'Thank you,' I said, hoping she could lipread. She shrugged and took the book down, and was ushered away by her sister and the dog to go and have their picnic. I waved and blew her a kiss.

That was when the second thing happened. Still puffy-faced and far too hot but feeling a bit cheered by the little girl's message, I got out of the car and sat on a nearby bench overlooking the park and the happy families. Some old dude appeared next to me and sat down, smoking a cigarette. He looked at the sea in the distance, inhaling the suffocating smoke and seemed content listening to the sound of laughter and squawking of seagulls. That is, until I accidentally coughed at the plumes of grossness emanating from his cancer stick.

'Guess it's not the merriest Christmas for you then,' he said.

I shifted uncomfortably. 'Not really.'

'Me neither.'

I was unsure how to respond. 'Sorry,' I tried.

'Don't be.'

I sniffed and pushed my hair out of my face. The guy ran a hand through his own curly hair, taking another drag and blowing the plume out of the side of his mouth. Maybe he wasn't that old. Mid thirties? He needed to shave. He scratched his nose and shifted in his seat before replying.

'They say Christmas is the loneliest time if you have no one.'

He tore his gaze away from the sea and looked at me. His eyes took in my hair, smudged make-up, accessories. 'You don't look like someone who has no one though,' he said.

'No,' I agreed somewhat reluctantly. 'But I *feel* like I have no one ... or ... I don't feel like a *someone*.'

'Who do you have?'

'I guess, my family. Mum, Dad, sister. But my parents don't seem to know I exist most of the time and my sister's crazy –'

The guy snorted.

'It's true!' I shouted. 'That's why I'm here, because she's in the crazy house at the hospital and now *she* doesn't seem to know I exist either!'

I stopped and took a breath, feeling overheated and

pissed off that this dude wasn't taking me seriously. He was looking at the sea again, squinting in the sun. The smoke from his cigarette caught in my throat and I coughed again.

'Must be pretty scary that your sister is so sick.'

'Yup,' I said.

'Must be pretty scary for your parents too.' He looked at me again.

I felt a pang of shame and looked down at my shoes. 'It's just … they have each other … and they're watching out for Cate. They don't *see* me. I'm walking through life totally invisible.'

His smoke was finished and he flicked it into the grass.

'So speak up,' he said, standing to leave. A ball landed at his feet and he picked it up and rolled it back to the little boy with the bad aim standing in the grass.

I was stunned into silence. I wanted to say something else to this guy, but nothing felt quite adequate. He grinned at me as he walked past.

'I hope you have a better Christmas next year.' He kept walking.

'Um, you too.'

He stopped abruptly and looked back at me.

'You need to find your own happiness, I reckon.'

'What?'

'Sometimes your joy is the source of your smile, but sometimes your smile can be the source of your joy.'

'What?'

The dude shrugged and kicked a tuft of grass. 'I dunno, I think it's some Buddhist quote. I've been meaning to test it on someone. Merry Christmas.'

I watched him as he crossed the street and walked straight into the same place I'd just come from: the psych unit.

'Merry Christmas,' I said quietly, but he'd already disappeared.

Twenty-eight

The drive home was thick with tension and the deafening sound of stony silence. Pamela Panic was rigid in the passenger seat, staring ahead of her, unseeing. Her eyes were as red and puffy as mine, and so far she hadn't said a word to me. Damn-it-all Dave's big hands gripped the steering wheel as he navigated the roads.

I switched on my iPod and tried to tune the world out. Still, all I could hear was the guy's words echoing in the walls of my mind. *Speak up*. It was basically what Alannah had said too. I knew I needed to. But what exactly was the right way to go about it? As for finding my own happiness, I had no idea how to go about that.

The car pulled up in our driveway, and my father had barely pulled up the handbrake before my mother flung her door open and climbed out, fumbling with the keys for the front door. I stayed seated in the car and watched wearily as my father got out too, closing his door with a bit too much force and stalked up the path. They both disappeared inside. Had they even remembered I was present?

Speaking of presents, I decided to be helpful and popped the boot to haul out the Christmas gifts and food that were sitting abandoned. After three trips, I'd carried everything in. The parentals were nowhere to be seen. Dragging the bag of presents over to the tree I unpacked them all and set them back up where they'd started. Maybe we could have Christmas anyway, I figured. Cate's presents I pushed to the back before switching the fairy lights on and walking over to where I'd left the food. I set the table and pulled out plates of cold chicken, rice salad, greek salad, French bread, ham, marinated feta and more. I filled up two wine glasses with wine and filled my own with orange juice (for show). I put some Christmas music on and sat on the couch, waiting.

I waited so long for them to come out of their respective rooms that I dozed off, and when I awoke the room was still empty and the CD had stopped. I looked at the dining room table, self-pity welling up in my eyes. Suddenly, I was furious. I knew it: this was the time to do it. This was the time to speak up.

I stood up so fast the room spun, and marched to Pamela's room – propelled by rage – lights exploding in my vision. She was lying on her bed staring blankly at the stupidly elaborate chandelier on the ceiling. Hers was the only room in the house with such a self-indulgent light fixture. I seethed with hatred towards her. Maybe it wasn't always about Queen Cate. Maybe it was actually all about Princess Pamela Panic. I stood in the doorway, my heart a jackhammer in its cage and she didn't even look at me. Took a shaky breath. Tried to steady myself.

'I put the lunch out.'

She sighed, all melancholy.

'I'm not hungry.'

I wanted to scream. I felt my face contorting, twisting up with the effort to keep the scream inside. I tried again.

'I put the lunch out an hour ago, Mother.'

'I said I'm not hungry, Sylvia. It's been a rough day.'

That. Was it.

'It's been a rough day?!!' I spat. 'Who has it been a rough day for, Pamela? All of us? Your precious Cate? Or just you? What about me, Pamela? WHAT ABOUT ME?!'

My mother was up now, charging around the bed towards me. I took off down the hall.

'Come back here and say that, Sylvia!' She was shrieking as she followed me to the lounge.

I stopped short at the dining table and flung my arm out wildly, like some overzealous, deranged game show host, at the food I'd laid out, the wine glasses filled.

'I did this for you!' I cried. 'Why can't we have Christmas anyway! It's *Christmas* for fuck's sake!'

Damn-it-all Dave appeared in the doorway, looking as though he'd just woken up. A startled frown creased his forehead. I hated him too.

'What are you doing?' He spoke more calmly than Pamela, who was standing stiff and tense, one hand on her hip, one hand at her temples, panic at fever pitch.

I looked at him defiantly. 'Speaking up! I don't even exist in this house! You're so caught up with my trainwreck of a sister you don't even ask me how I am! It makes me *sick* to think you've raised me to be invisible! I'll never be as good as your little *Catherine*, even though she's sick and crazy! You have *no idea* what I've been going through night after fucking night when you're off visiting her.'

I was choking on my words.

'Now just calm down, Sylvie,' Dave tried. 'Maybe you need to walk this off. Go get some fresh air.'

Tears rolled down my face and my breaths were ragged.

'I shouldn't have to.' I sobbed. 'I live here too. Why do I have to disappear all the time?'

Pamela was advancing on me.

'How dare you,' she hissed. 'How *dare* you accuse me of not knowing what's going on with my own daughter. You're an attention seeker!'

I had no handle on my fury now. Without any real

conscious thought, I pulled my sleeve up and held my arm out. The red drained out of her face.

'Do you *really* know what's going on with me, Mother?'

The slap took my ragged breath away. It was short and sharp but there was power to it that left my cheek with a sting for hours afterwards. Straight after her hand had made contact with my face she fell backwards – *or did I push her?* – into the dining chairs. I was aware of an expletive from Dave and my heart beating like a drum in my ears. My cheek felt like a layer of skin had been stripped off it.

I put my hand up, expecting to feel blood, or skin bubbling away as if doused with corrosive chemicals, but it felt smooth as usual. As though in a fog, where I seemed to spend most of my time these days, I grabbed my bag which had been discarded by the front door, and ran outside and down the path, feet pounding the concrete.

'Sylvie!'

Something in Dave's voice made me stop and turn towards it. He stood on the porch. 'Where are you going?'

'I don't know,' I sniffed. 'Maybe Belle's.'

He nodded but made no move to stop me.

'Let me know when you get there. And for the love of God, Sylvia, keep yourself safe.'

Twenty-nine

Hail Mary! Buses run at Christmas after all. I climbed on board, surprised to see more passengers than I expected. Most people were smiling and the overall vibe was a warm one. I wiped sweat off my forehead and took a seat.

At the next stop, the bus stooped so an old lady could climb on. After studying the seats, she chose one and made her way over to it. Her grey hair was swept back into a bun, and some strands had come free in the humid day, falling around her face and framing it in a modern, youthful way. She was wearing a skirt in a pale, minty green, and the matching light jacket was slung over her arm. She wore practical white sandals and carried a bunch of bright flowers. Her glasses sat on her nose and were attached to a delicate chain so she wouldn't lose them. She smiled happily as she went past and took her seat right behind me.

The bus was moving again. I watched as we passed through the village, eyeing all the closed shops which had been deserted in favour of family and friends. Adam's pizza place was closed. I kept my eyes on it until I could see it no more, wondering again what he was doing, and if I ever crossed his mind.

I jumped approximately a foot in the air when my phone rang, the sound blaring throughout the bus. I fumbled in my bag, searching for the sound. My hand found it and I pulled it out, reading the name on the screen. I hit the button to answer and held it up to my ear.

'Hi, Belle.' I was aware of the dull tone in my voice.

'Sylvie! Are you okay? Your dad rang my mum and said you're coming over here?'

'Huh? My dad rang your mum … do they know each other?'

'Nope!'

Behind Belle, people were laughing. A child was singing 'Jingle Bells'.

'Then how did he get her number?'

'No idea,' Belle laughed. 'But are you okay? How far away are you?'

'Oh … I don't think I'll come over actually. I just told Dad that to get him off my case.'

'Don't be dumb, we're expecting you. And besides, if you don't show up Mum will ring your dad back and they'll send out a search party!'

I giggled.

'Get off at Sherman Drive and I'll meet you.'

'Okay, I'm probably ten minutes away.'

'I'll leave now!' She ended the call and I returned my phone to my bag.

'It sounds like you have a loyal friend there,' a voice behind me said.

I turned in my seat and found the old woman leaning forward, as if she wanted to share a secret with me.

'Uh, I do. Thanks.'

'Going to share Christmas with her family, are you? Forgive me, dear, I couldn't help overhearing.'

What an eavesdropper!

'Yeah …'

The woman smiled kindly.

'That's very generous of her. Have you been friends for long?'

'Only this year, really. We're in the same English class.'

What the hell? So nosy!

'Sounds like she's one to hold on to. People come into our lives for a reason you know. Even if it's only for a short time.'

I nodded politely. 'Are you going to visit family?'

Her face lit up behind her glasses. 'Why yes as a matter of fact I am! I'm going to visit my new great-grandson! My first one! He's the apple of my eye. My husband passed away last year and it's really been a trying time. I'm just thrilled with this new life.'

I smiled at her. 'Congratulations. You look lovely.'

'Oh thank you, you sweet girl. I have so few occasions to dress up for these days.'

Her smile had traces of sadness at the edges and for a moment her eyes were far away.

'This is my stop,' she said suddenly and pushed the button. 'You have a good time with your friend and make sure you keep her. Not everyone is so lucky at Christmas.'

'Have a nice time with your family,' I said, watching her collect her jacket, handbag and flowers.

Maybe it was intuition, or maybe our unspoken sadness momentarily connected, but as she stood, something clicked.

'Sometimes your joy is the source of your smile, and sometimes your smile can be the source of your joy.' I started it off sketchily and then ran through the last part too quickly, hoping I'd got it right.

The woman looked kind of taken aback by my sudden wisdom. But her expression quickly changed into a smile that gave me a glimpse of what she would've looked like when she was younger. 'That's beautiful, dear. Is it from a book?'

I shrugged, like the guy in the park had. 'I think it's a Buddhist thing. Just wanted to try it out on someone.'

The bus jerked to a stop and the lady nodded as she tried to steady herself. 'Well, it's just what I needed to hear. Thank you.'

When I jumped off the bus, Belle threw her arms around me in a tight hug. I laughed despite everything that had happened that day. The old lady was right. Belle was the only thing holding me up right now.

'Merry Christmas, Sylv,' she said, pulling away and studying my face. 'Mum says you've had a pretty rubbish day.' She linked her arm through mine and led me in the direction of her house.

'What exactly did Dad tell her?'

'Just about your sister. He said you went to visit her today and it didn't go well, and that things are a bit tense between you and your mum, and was it all right if you visited us.'

'That was the tactful story.'

'What's the uncut version?'

Belle's bare arm, linked through mine was sitting right on top of my cutting handiwork. Her skin brushed the fabric of my sleeve and I felt a pang of jealousy. It was boiling. When would I be able to wear short sleeves again? Belle of the Books was waiting for me to answer, her magnified eyes ever watchful, hair blowing softly in the gentle breeze. I so badly wanted to be her at that moment.

'I'll tell you later,' I said.

Thirty

Belle's house had a white picket fence that said 'Everglade' on a little plaque set into the gate. She led me up the little stone path, and up the steps to the house, which had the cutest little porch with a rocking chair and small table. The window in the front door was stained-glass, for crying out loud.

When Belle opened the door we were standing at the end of a long wooden hallway that must have been a century old. I hadn't been to Belle's house much. She hadn't been to mine once, because of the whole Cate thing.

The smell of cooking hit me and my stomach rumbled. I hadn't eaten all day.

'Dinner's not for a couple of hours but there's still plenty of food out to snack on,' Belle was telling me as she led me down the hallway and up the stairs. Had she *heard* my stomach?! I had to suppress a groan. I felt so pathetic. There I was, accepting charity from my only friend and her family because my own family didn't want me.

Belle opened her bedroom door. 'Put your bag in here.'

I stepped inside and gasped. 'Holy Huckleberry! Isobel! When did you do your room up?'

'My parents let me do it up for my birthday.'

I was standing in the room of a gypsy princess. The walls were painted white with one rich purple feature wall. Her bed sat in the corner with a beautiful canopy of colourful fabrics, which hung suspended from the ceiling and were pulled back and tucked behind the headboard. Next to her bed was a small ladder acting as a bedside table. It had a satin robe draped over one side and books stacked on the steps, along with the case for her glasses and a small lamp. At the foot of the bed were a couple of old suitcases stacked on top of each other. A cosy-looking chair sat by the window.

Fairy lights adorned the window frame and the main light in the centre of the ceiling hung low, with a red vintage light shade. On the walls were black and white pictures of people, carefully framed and obviously admired. I looked at Belle, a question on my face.

'Authors,' she replied. She was grinning, enjoying me liking her room.

Of course. Literary love aside, this room was home

to a Belle I didn't even know. Momentarily, I was lost for words.

I put my bag down as footsteps sounded on the stairs. The door creaked slightly and then, 'This must be Sylvie!'

I turned to face a woman about the same age as my mother wearing a white singlet and a long red skirt, bare feet, and with a wild mane of lush dark hair roughly swept back in a ponytail. She had Belle's beautiful eyes.

'Hello,' I said, feeling shy.

She was super stunning, for a mum. A workaholic, according to Belle – which is why I'd never met her – but a beautiful one. I'd been expecting someone who looked tired and frazzled, like Pamela.

'Valerie,' she said, and pulled me into a hug.

'Mum!' Belle protested. Valerie smelt like spices and baking. I loved her already. 'You've just met her. You'll freak her out.'

'Oh don't be stupid, Belle. It's Christmas.' She held me by the arms and studied me. 'I'm sorry to hear you're having a hard time today.' She led me out of Belle's haven and down the stairs.

I had to ask. 'Um, how did my dad get your phone number? Do you know each other?'

'No, lovely,' Valerie laughed. 'I'm on the school board of trustees and your dad's friends with the chair. They work together, I understand. Your dad sounds like a very astute man though, Sylvie. I'm sure he could get anyone's details if he wanted to.'

Dave: 1.

Sylvia: 0.

I was led into the kitchen, with Belle trailing behind.

'We do everything in the kitchen in this house,' Valerie said, as she waved people over to meet me.

Two women about Valerie's age were cutting up vegetables and stirring pots while snacking on chips and dip. Aunties. They smiled at me and said hello. One of them offered me a glass of ginger beer which I accepted gratefully. Belle had a large family and they all seemed to be there. It was becoming increasingly apparent to me that I knew barely anything about my most loyal friend.

I knew her as an only child, but here billions of little cousins crowded around her, demanding that she entertain them. We walked out into the backyard which had the most beautiful blue flowers, and a bunch of men sitting around a couple of picnic tables drinking beer. Uncles, apparently, and Belle's dad, who was wearing shorts and had a face full of whiskers. He was picking casually at a guitar. I remembered Belle mentioning once that he was in some kind of band. He offered his hand and I shook it.

'Andrew,' he said. 'Well, Merry Christmas. Are you staying for dinner?'

I looked at Belle.

'Of course she is!' said Belle.

'If that's okay?' I said.

He smiled jovially. Possibly a little bit 'merrily'. His eyelids had a slightly heavy look to them.

'Of course it is! You're welcome to stay as long as you like, Sylvie.'

A wave of relief washed over me as he turned his attention back to his guitar.

'Come and see our fort!' A little girl said, grabbing my hand and pulling me with her.

'This is Alice,' Belle said. 'My bossiest cousin.'

I was dragged over to a corner where trees stood in a cluster. Draped over the branches were sheets and blankets creating a little shelter, and on the grass were cushions and pillows.

'Wowzer!' I said. 'This is amazing!'

All the kids crowded around us as we settled onto the pillows. Seemed I was a bit of a novelty. After a couple of minutes of tireless chatter about dolls and planes and 'Look at me! Look at this!', Belle's aunt Minnie came over and ushered them away.

'Leave the big girls alone for a while,' she said, rolling her eyes at us.

'This is awesome, Belle. Thank you so much for taking me in.'

'Don't be stupid, Sylvie. What happened today?'

I took a deep breath and told her everything. Belle displayed all the appropriate reactions – wide eyes, gasps, exclamations ('she didn't recognise you?!') and at the end she sighed and said, 'Well that blows.'

'Don't I know it.' I looked over at her. 'Can I be your sister? I don't want to go home ever again.'

Belle laughed. 'You can stay the night! We could go to the Boxing Day sales tomorrow.'

'I don't have much money, but that sounds fun,' I said. 'Thanks. Also, why has it taken this long for me to meet your parents? I love them!'

'Don't know. Mum works late at her salon a bit. And Dad's in the studio a lot or touring sometimes. But you never come over much anyway.'

'What did you say his band's called?'

Belle of the Books rolled her eyes.

'Reckless Abandon. It's super old-school. They were big in like the 90s but they still do gigs around the place now. He leaves to do the summer tour the day after Boxing Day.'

'I want to see them play some time! You're so lucky to have a dad like that.'

'He's my stepdad actually. My real dad left when I was five.'

'Really? Why have you never mentioned this before? Do you still see him?'

'You didn't ask. And no,' she shook her head. 'He wasn't very nice.'

'I'm sorry. I really had no idea.'

'It's okay,' Belle sat up. 'Let's go see if we can help with anything.'

I ate so much food I felt like I was going to go into

a food coma. Belle's family were amazing cooks and served up four roast chickens, one ham, dishes full of vegetable casseroles, and a rainbow of salads. When it was time for dessert my plate was piled up with pavlova and peaches, ice cream and more cream. Belle and I sat at the adults' table while the young cousins staged a food fight at theirs.

After we helped clear up, we sat outside on cushions and chairs with blankets, and sang songs led by Andrew on the guitar. I watched the cousins getting sleepier and sleepier as they dozed on whatever surface they could find, eyes heavy – reluctantly closing and then snapping open, resisting sleep. Gradually their parents began lifting their sleepy little bodies and carrying them to the car before returning to say their goodbyes. Every one of them said goodbye to me. Every single one. This was a place where I was visible. I was sorry to see them all go but the roller coaster day was catching up to me and I was aware of my limbs feeling weary too. I followed Belle to her room where she hauled out a trundle bed from under her own and began collecting pillows and blankets for me.

'I don't have a toothbrush!' I yawned.

'Ew! We'll sort it tomorrow,' she said as she threw the blankets on the mattress. I helped her straighten them up.

'Thanks so much for letting me crash your Christmas, Belle,' I said. 'It's the best Christmas I've ever had.' And I meant it.

Thirty-one

Valerie drove us to my place in the morning. I was hesitant to face the parents, but I was only going to brush my teeth and collect the money I knew I would have in a card from my grandparents. Valerie and Belle accompanied me to the door.

'I'd like to meet your dad if that's okay, Sylvie,' Valerie smiled at me kindly. I smiled back. This was a safe person.

'That's fine, but be warned – he's really weird.'

Valerie laughed a deep husky laugh. 'All parents are. Right, Belle?'

Belle rolled her eyes behind her spectacles. 'Right again, Mother.'

Together we walked up the path and I put my key in the front door. Pushing it open I stepped tentatively over the threshold and said in a small voice, half hoping they wouldn't be home, 'Hello?'

A noise from down the hall and Damn-it-all Dave appeared, freshly showered, smelling of shampoo and aftershave. He registered my presence and hesitated briefly, arm half extended towards me as if to hug me. I shrank back and watched sadness ripple across his face. He quickly rearranged his expression and extended his hand instead towards Valerie.

'This must be Belle and Valerie.'

I left the parents to make small talk and chat about serious parent stuff while I dragged Belle to my room.

'Welcome to my lair,' I said dramatically, clearing off space for her to sit on the chair while I grabbed a change of clothes. 'Wait there, I'll just be a sec,' I said over my shoulder, as I headed for the bathroom. Coming to a sudden halt in the doorway of my room, I spun around again to face her. She blinked at me.

'It's nothing like your amazing room,' I told her. *Like she couldn't see that for herself.* I suddenly felt flooded with shame. What must she think of me?

She just shook her head. 'If you pulled the curtains, and let some sunlight in, it would be really nice.' She jumped up and opened the still partially derailed curtains. My room was filled with light.

I felt such a mixture of emotions at that moment: ashamed, sad, lucky, undeserving.

'You're too nice to me,' is all I said.

With my clothes changed and teeth brushed I led Belle back out to the lounge, where my father was entertaining Valerie. He cleared his throat and stood, handing me the card with money from my grandparents.

'They're in the Caribbean,' he explained to Valerie. He pressed some more cash of his own into my hand.

'Thanks,' I said dully.

'Have fun shopping.' He cleared his throat again and his mouth moved silently. It seemed to be forming words he wasn't sure he could say aloud. Then he spoke. 'Your Mother ... has gone to stay in a hotel for a couple of nights. Will you stay at home tonight?'

I think I may have been unintentionally imitating a goldfish because he looked at me standing before him, mouth agape and said, 'You don't have to. Valerie has said you can stay at their place again if you like but ... It would be nice to see you.'

He was all alone at Christmas time. It wasn't even that he didn't have a family. It was that his family was in pieces. I took a breath.

'Okay, I'll stay.'

He didn't bother to conceal his relief. 'I'll cook something nice.'

The mall was packed full of cashed-up shoppers looking feverishly for bargains. Valerie, Belle and I were swallowed into the surging tidal wave the second we stepped inside, and my ears were filled with fragments of strangers' conversations.

Valerie caught my eye and grinned. She cupped

her hand around her mouth and yelled, 'I'll meet you back here at twelve!'

Belle and I nodded and parted ways with Valerie, focused on retail therapy.

'Where to first?' I asked Belle and she made a beeline for the bookshop. My patience waned as she delved further and further into the shelves, and after flipping through magazines and reading the back of some novels, I could no longer even see her. I got out my phone and sent a text.

Me: Going to look at clothes.
Txt u up later.

Belle: Ok I won't be long.

Liar.

I got lost in the shops but nothing was jumping out at me. I walked through picking a few items off racks here and there, my anxiety increasing as the money burnt a searing hole through my pocket. I wanted to treat myself. I wanted something nice. But I wasn't feeling inspired. I was about to walk out of the shop when I felt someone grasp my upper arm. Belle.

'Did you lose your fingers in my batwings?' I said, and turned, expecting to see her laughing and holding enough books to fill a library. Instead, what I saw was … Adam. With a bemused look on his face. My stomach fell to approximately 200 metres below sea level, and I tried my old trick of making a quick inventory of appropriate ways to die in a shopping mall. He realised he was still holding my arm and released it quickly. He wiggled his fingers.

'Um, nope, fingers all accounted for.'

I laughed and mentally smacked myself in the head. *Play it cool, Sylvie.*

Awkward silence.

We just stood there, opposite each other, people winding their way around us, chaos reigning in the storm of sales, and in the eye of it I felt connected to him, and I was sure he felt it too. Someone behind me knocked me forwards, and the invisible wall between us dissolved as he put his arm out to steady me.

He held onto my arm. Again. He didn't let go.

'How was your Christmas?' he asked.

Every synapse in my body was exploding with electricity. I thought I might spontaneously combust.

'Um, it was good actually. I spent it at Belle's house.'

He looked, understandably, a little surprised. 'Oh, that's cool …'

'Yeah, um … How was yours?'

He brushed his hand through his hair.

I couldn't imagine ever touching him so casually.

'…Good,' he was saying as I forced myself to stop gazing at his hair. 'My older brother came back from uni and brought his girlfriend, and my sister just had twins a couple of months ago, so there was a lot of crying and baby voices going on –'

'You're an uncle?'

'Yeah, scary eh?'

'No, it's awesome.'

I meant it. I had never stopped to consider all the different hats that my glorious crush might wear. To me, he was just Adam, the object of my desire, the guy for whom I'd created an imaginary shrine in my head. But he was also an uncle, a son, a brother, a friend. And here he was, taking the time to come and talk to … me?

He was looking at me carefully. I remembered I hadn't even put on my make-up in the morning, since Belle and Valerie had been waiting for me. I knew I should feel awkward but for some reason I didn't.

It was like he was seeing *me*. For the second time. And he wasn't running away. He hesitated and my heart skipped a beat. *Maybe he is going to run away. Maybe he's just trying to find his feet.* He cleared his throat. No, he was trying to find his voice. His eyes started looking everywhere but at me.

'Would you like to go see a movie sometime?'

Holy. Shit.

I thought I might faint.

'Yeah!' I squeaked. *Squeaked!* He didn't seem to notice the strangled pitch.

'Sweet.' He gave me his phone and I dutifully entered my number, checking it a thousand times to make sure it was right, hands shaking as though my body had its own richter scale. I handed it back to him, sure I was going to drop it.

'Thanks,' he said. 'I'll text you.'

'Okay,' I breathed.

He turned to walk away, and then turned back, an afterthought on his lips. My heart hesitated.

Here it is. This is where he tells me he was joking.

'You look pretty with no make-up.'

What?

'You look more like you.'

I had no words. I just smiled and he smiled back, and then turned and was swallowed by the crowd.

My phone beeped.

Belle: Where are you?

Me: Over the moon! Meet u at
the coffee shop. BIG NEWS!!!!!!!

My phone beeped again.

Unknown number: Hey it's Adam.
Just checkin u gave me the right #...

I had to fight the urge to jump for joy.

Thirty-two

Valerie and Belle dropped me home after our shopping excursion. I had armloads of fashion-filled shopping bags and a smile plastered across my face.

'See you tomorrow, Sylvie. We'll pick you up on the way back from dropping off Andrew.'

'Thank you so much!' I bubbled. 'I'll see you then!'

I waved as they drove away and then skipped up the drive. I didn't even care that I was back home. I opened the door and was met with the smell of cooking. Following my nose to the kitchen, bags anchoring my arms to my sides, I found my dad bending down looking in the oven. He was cooking a roast, his signature dish. He closed the oven door and smiled warily at me, as if I might bite when approached.

'Hey, Dad.'

'Hi, Sylvie. Looks like you had a successful day.' He observed the numerous bags slung over my arms. 'Roast should be ready soon. You've got time to put your new things away, though. Do you want a lemonade?'

What the hell? He was being so nice.

Emotions flipped through me rapidly, much like you flip through DVDs in the bargain bin, trying to find the right one. He was looking at me expectantly, waiting for a response.

'Got any Coke?'

He immediately spun on his heel and walked to the fridge.

'Coke. Yes, we have Coke.' He went about getting a glass and filling it up as I went to my room.

I closed the door and emptied the contents of my bags on the bed. Then picking each item up, one by one, I folded them and put them in piles. I congratulated myself that not one of the items was black. Not one of them was a corset or a short skirt. I'd bought a new pair of jeans, some tops, a couple of dresses and a hoodie. They were clothes the old Sylvie would wear. The Sylvie I hadn't wanted to be. The Sylvie I wanted back.

It had been Belle's idea. 'If it's you he really likes, then show him you!'

I'd picked out my date outfit. *Was it a date?* Maybe he just wanted to hang out, like friends. Doubt flickered. What if he just meant he preferred me without make-up? What if he still liked the skanky clothing style I'd adopted? Belle had shaken her head at me.

'No, dopey,' she'd said. 'He doesn't like the same Sylvie that Chris liked.'

Chris. The name evoked immediate feelings of loathing and anxiety. The Facebook storm seemed to have blown through; people forgetting with the excitement of Christmas and the summer holidays. I wasn't sure I'd got away with it though, and the thought occurred to me that Adam would be disgusted if he found out it was me. Another anxiety tugged. *What if Adam has the same expectations as Chris had?* I tried to shake it off but it was insidious, following me everywhere, taunting.

Valerie was going to do my hair. They were going to pick me up after they'd dropped Andrew off at the airport for his summer tour, and then she was going to work her magic. I was seeing Adam the day after and the plan was that my hair would look more as it used to.

'It might not be quite what you want, mind,' Valerie had warned. 'You've got quite a lot of warmth from the red left in there and it could be a challenge to get rid of it.'

'So it could go horribly wrong?'

'Don't worry,' Belle grinned. 'My mum knows what she's doing.'

Dad knocked on my door.

'Sylvie? Are you in there?'

I yanked the door open and he looked surprised.

'Oh good. I thought you'd done a runner.'

I followed him down the hall and found the table set for two with the roast chicken and vegetables laid out. Despite having eaten to full capacity the day before at Belle's house, my mouth began watering as soon as the smell reached my senses. I loved my dad's roasts. It'd been a long time.

He'd turned on the Christmas tree lights and put on some Christmas music. My presents, still unopened, were laid out under the tree. It could almost have been a regular Christmas Day, except it was Boxing Day and just the two of us.

'This is nice,' I said, seating myself at the table and immediately reaching for the serving spoons.

My dad shrugged it off as if he made such thoughtful gestures all the time.

'We've all been having a rough time lately. May as well try and keep our heads up.'

I lifted my glass of Coke. 'To a better Christmas next year.'

He lifted his beer bottle and clinked it against my glass. 'I'll drink to that.'

We chatted sporadically throughout the meal about school, exams, friends, work, weather; awkwardly tiptoeing around the things that mattered – my mother, my sister, sexual assault, the cuts on my arm.

Afterwards we cleared up the dishes and loaded them into the dishwasher.

'I could get used to this,' I said, and then, 'How long is Pamela staying away for?'

I could see his shoulders tense. He leaned on the counter, as if it could help hold all the weight he was carrying.

'I was wondering when you were going to ask that. I don't know, to be honest. Some time away will do her good, though. She should go and get a manicure, or whatever it is women do when they're stressed. She doesn't take care of herself …' He ran a hand through his hair, salt and pepper at the edges. His eyes met mine.

'Are you sad, Dad?'

'A little.'

I didn't know how to deal with fatherly feelings, and found myself repeating the random smoking dude's words again, since they were such a hit with the old woman. 'I reckon you both need to find your own happiness.'

He raised his eyebrows at me wryly. 'This from the queen of merriment.'

I decided to overlook the sarcasm and nodded sagely. 'Sometimes your joy is the source of your smile and sometimes your smile can be the source of your joy.'

It didn't appear to be working on him the way it worked on the old lady.

'Where the hell are you getting this stuff from?'

'I think it's a Buddhist quote.'

He shook his head and had another sip of beer. 'The things they teach in schools these days.'

'Someone should try it on Pamela, and see what she says.'

'I already know what she'd say.'

'Why didn't I get my tubes tied?'

'Sylvie. She'd say that you're the source of her joy. And her smile.'

'But I make her so angry.'

'Because she loves you so much.'

I snorted like some kind of farm animal. 'She has a funny way of showing it.'

Dad handed me a bowl of Christmas pudding with extra cream.

'Do you love her?' he asked.

'Well, yeah, obviously. She's my mother.'

He licked cream off his finger and picked up his own bowl.

'You have a funny way of showing it,' was all he said.

We sat in the lounge, me sprawled on the couch, Dad reclining in his chair, watching some Christmas movie on TV. We'd opened our presents. He had considerably less than I did which made me feel sad. He shrugged it off.

'It's just what happens when you're an adult,' he said. 'It doesn't mean you're loved any less, it just means you want less for yourself and more for your kids.'

I mulled this over. 'So ... You want stuff for me and Cate?'

He took a swig of beer.

'Of course, doofus. You're our beloved daughters,' he said.

'What *do* you want? Like … in particular?'

He suddenly looked old. Like he'd been photo-shopped right before my eyes.

'I want Cate to be better, obviously, and I want you to be happy. Find your own happiness or whatever. And I want you to stop cutting your arms up. You'll regret that when you have to explain to your kids why they look like they got stuck in a shredder.'

His words were like my mother's slap, although I wasn't sure if he meant for them to be. I felt the sting, intended or not. Words can hurt like that.

On screen, a dude had knocked on his best friend's door and was telling his bestie's wife, using signs, that she was perfect. I craved for Adam to tell me I was perfect. But I wasn't. Nursing my wounded feelings, I stood up.

'Thanks for dinner and my presents, Dad. I'm going to Belle's tomorrow. Night.'

I felt his eyes on me as I left the room, but I didn't turn around.

Thirty-three

'Now the clouds have gone and all the rain: it's a sky-blue kind of day ...'

Belle was singing to the stereo and dancing around me as I sat on the stool with a plastic cape around my shoulders. I was trying to watch her but my eyes could only reach so far, and whenever I tried to move my head Valerie would tug my hair and tell me to keep still.

'All those things that make it hard to see,' sang Belle. 'Now it's nothing but sunshine – bright, bright sunshine – for you and me ...'

I was learning that there was always music playing at Belle's house. I wanted to get up and dance with her. This song in particular made me so happy. It was a hit for Andrew's band back in the old days. I felt cautiously hopeful. Maybe the clouds were clearing. I hummed along to the music and wished I was Belle's sister.

But it wasn't all milk and honey being Belle, I reminded myself frequently now. She had said her biological father wasn't very nice. Valerie had gone through a divorce and rebuilt her life. I watched my friend sling her arm across Valerie's shoulders as the two of them surveyed my new 'do'. They were happy, smiling, singing. I thought they were two of the most inspiring women I'd ever met.

'Perfect!' Valerie exclaimed.

'It looks wicked, Sylvie!' Belle said.

Valerie whipped the cape from my shoulders and I hopped down from the stool with a numb bum. Belle carried over a mirror. I took it from her and my mouth dropped open. It was almost the old me. The hair was a little bit darker than my natural mousey brown, it had to be to cover the warmth from the red – Valerie had forewarned me. And she'd cut my hair. Up to my chin. I shook my head slightly and watched the way my hair moved with it. I felt lighter.

For such a casual woman, Valerie had cut my hair with careful precision. An architect of hair styling. Her apron had rustled as she moved around me, whipping the comb out of the apron pocket and dropping it back in again. Her silver bangles clanged in my ears. With my hair cut short, I felt renewed. I was leaving a part of me behind.

Maybe now she would recognise me.

I hadn't heard how Cate was doing. I knew Pamela Panic and my father had both gone to visit her on Boxing Day, and that they had prearranged the time so they didn't have to see each other. I wondered if it would confuse Cate that our parents would now start visiting separately. Was she better or worse?

'She has good days and bad days,' was all Dad would say that morning when I'd asked. 'Christmas Day was a particularly bad one. They didn't think she'd been taking her meds. Now she is watched more closely, and has been put on an injection for the time being.'

I had no idea what all this stuff really meant. I didn't know what her meds were or what they did. I didn't really even understand her illness. Schizoaffective disorder. I could barely even spell it.

'Is she ever coming home?' I said.

'When she's better,' Dad said through a mouthful of toast.

Belle and Valerie dropped me home again and I ran inside and straight to my room. The butterflies that had been fluttering in my stomach all day were in full force and I felt giddy with excitement and anticipation. And apprehension. I eyed up the outfit I had chosen for my date/whatever-it-was with Adam. I put it on and looked at myself critically in the mirror. I was almost the 'old' Sylvie. But was the old Sylvie what Adam wanted?

All at once I felt the weight of Chris crushing me again, the smell of his clammy hand clamped over my mouth. It took my breath away. I backed up and sat on the bed, breathing deeply, trying to quell the nausea and panic that were turning over inside.

'Pull yourself together, Sylvie the Second,' I whispered.

I shut my eyes and imagined the sea, the sun warming me, the waves carrying me, the breeze whispering to me, and eventually I became aware of my pulse dropping to a steady thrum, and my breath moving in and out of my lungs with more ease. I opened my eyes, stood up and made my way back to the mirror.

One last check.

Adam would be here any minute. I was wearing a long-sleeved blue-and-white-striped dress with tights, and pink slip-on flats. I felt comfortable. If we ate, I would be able to manage more than a couple of bites since I wouldn't have to worry about looking three-months pregnant every time I exhaled. I hoped Adam would like me too.

I chewed my fingernails, which Belle had painted pink and blue while we waited for my hair to process.

'Don't screw this up,' I said to my reflection.

The doorbell rang. I froze. I could hear my dad's footsteps heading for the front door, and I realised just then that I'd never actually told him I was going on a date. Propelled into urgent action, I flew down the hall, swooping in front of Dad, who had just found a boy standing on his doorstep asking for his daughter. He appeared slightly confused, looking around as if he hadn't realised he had one.

'Hi Dad, bye Dad, this is Adam, we're going out for a bit,' I said in a rush, dragging Adam from the porch and heading down the drive. I glanced back, and instead of seeing my father irate, jumping up and down on the porch yelling, 'Damn it all!' and a variety of expletives, he was staring at me in something that kind of resembled wonder. He pulled his cell phone out of his pocket. Mine rang.

'Here we go,' I said, out of breath. I answered it. 'Dad.'

'Where are you going and what time will you be home?'

'We're going to a movie and will be home by ten o'clock, I promise.'

The line was quiet.

'Have fun.'

Silence.

'You look nice, Sylvie.'

'Cringe, Dad. Bye.'

I ended the call.

'You look nice,' Adam said. 'I'm impressed. It's the old Sylvie again. But with shorter hair.'

The compliment felt less cringe-worthy when he said it.

'My sister cut her hair off,' I said. 'So I wanted to as well.' Then I realised what I was babbling and looked at my feet, horrified.

He just laughed.

'That's cool. Sisters in solidarity.'

I wanted to swing from the stars.

'Yeah!' I giggled. 'We're pretty tight.'

We walked a few more steps in silence.

'No scooter?'

'Nah, I can't take passengers. I usually like to leave getting pulled over by the cops for the second date.'

Will there be a second date? I'd never actually heard a hyena laugh before, but I was pretty sure that's what I sounded like.

'I thought we'd get dinner first. Is that okay with you?' he said.

'Yup, I'm starving.'

Ohmigod! Pig.

'I mean, I could eat …'

He lifted his head and looked at me and I thought I might drop dead.

'Sweet.'

I walked alongside him, perfectly content in his company, not taking much notice of where we were going and suddenly I registered that we had come to a stop outside Adam's work.

'Wait here,' he told me, and ducked inside.

Two minutes later he walked back out, holding two pizza boxes and two small bottles of Coke. He handed me the Cokes and grinned.

'Preorder perks! Follow me.'

His spare hand grabbed mine and he led me up the road and around the corner. I allowed myself to be led, not bothering to consider how he just knew I would like a whole pizza, not caring how unglamorous I would look eating a pizza in front of him, not worrying that he might be leading me to some gross alleyway where he would suddenly turn into Chris. There was only one thing on my mind. WE WERE HOLDING HANDS, PEOPLE!!! Where was *E! News* when you needed them?

He took me to the park and scanned it before finding a place to sit on a grassy hill. Down below, a crowd gathered around the gazebo to watch a local band play as part of the Summer Sounds festival.

'Sorry, I should've brought a blanket or something.'

'Oh no,' I said. 'I'm warm enough!'

'I meant to sit on …'

'Oh.'

He handed me a pizza box and flipped open his own.

'If you were cold I'd just give you my jacket.'

Squeeeeeeeeeee!

I was smiling so widely as I opened my pizza box that he asked what was wrong with me.

'Oh, um, nothing! It's just funny that you know what pizza to get me.'

'Same one you always get!' he laughed. 'I'd be sleeping on the job if I didn't know that by now.'

I looked at the slice of pizza in my hand doubtfully. Sliced mushrooms were nestled in amongst melted cheese.

'I eat it too much.'

He rolled his eyes.

'Don't be like that. I like a girl I can eat a pizza with.'

'Really?'

'Yes! Eat!'

So I did. Just like that. I devoured it, although not as quickly as he managed to. He seemed pleased. When he stood and carried the boxes over to the bin I surveyed the place he'd chosen for us to sit. It was in full view of people. There were families having picnics and takeaways, people running with their dogs, music lovers listening to the band in a gazebo lit up with fairy lights. He hadn't chosen somewhere secluded, where we would be hidden, like Chris had. Did he know? I didn't even really care. I felt like I was going to go whizzing off in deranged circles like a balloon that'd been let go.

He lay down next to me so I lay down too, and we watched dusk change the colour of the sky.

'So, tell me about yourself,' I ventured.

He burst out laughing.

'What is this? A job interview?'

I looked over at him.

'No,' I said. 'I don't really know anything about you. Apart from where you work and that you have an older brother at uni and a sister with twins which makes you an uncle ...'

He snorted. *Like I do!*

'Well that's more than a lot of people know!'

206

'But I want to know about *you!*' I protested. 'What's your favourite colour? What's your favourite subject? What are your hobbies? What do you want to do when you leave school? All those kinds of things …'

He chuckled, took a breath and exhaled slowly as he considered my barrage of questions.

'Green. Science. My hobbies include listening to music, video games, cricket and being interrogated by the Spanish Inquisition led by Sylvie Rivers.'

My turn to burst into laughter. He laughed with me and I watched his chest shake with it. Once the laughter stopped bubbling up out of him he thought for a minute.

'I guess I don't really know what I want to do when I leave school yet. I'd like to be an engineer, I think.' He looked at the blanket of sky above us. The stars were just waking up.

'What I'd really love to be is an astronaut. But that would never happen.'

'Why not? Lately it seems like anything can happen.'

He turned his head to the side and studied me. I blushed and put a hand up to my face, looked away.

'Maybe,' he said. 'Anyway, what about you? Can I interrogate you now?'

And so I told him. I opened up about Cate and the parentals, and basically told him way too much information. At the end I stopped and eyed him closely, afraid he would freak out and run away. But he didn't. He just looked up at the sky.

'Jeez. Talk about a rough time.'

'Sorry for rambling,' I said. 'It's not really as bad as it sounds. You don't have to stick around, though. You know … now you know my family are a pack of whack jobs.'

And then he held my hand again. I repeat: *and then he held my hand again!!* My heart actually stopped.

'I'm okay here,' was all he said.

And my heart surged back into life with such a bang I gasped.

Do I really need to point out that we missed the movie? We stayed lying on the grass until all the people had left the park, the band was packing up and the sky had turned ink-stain black. My hand remained in his the entire time as we talked about everything and nothing, and when we realised there were clouds rolling in and felt sprinkles of rain on our hot skin, he stood at last and pulled me up.

'Ten o'clock curfew wasn't it?'

'Yup.'

'Well it's quarter to, so we'd better run!'

We tore through the streets hand in hand, laughing and panting. The rain, which had started as a sprinkle, seemed to be getting heavier with each step, so we sprinted across roads and hid under awnings all the way back to my place. It was under one of the awnings that it happened. He was running along, pulling me behind him, when he stopped suddenly and I almost slammed into him. Before I even fully registered what was happening his lips were on mine.

My eyes flew open wide in surprise until I saw that his were shut and so I dutifully closed mine too. An internal struggle began between wanting to get lost in the moment and wanting to appear graceful at the same time. His mouth was surprisingly soft and I hoped mine was too. I seriously hoped I was doing it right.

This, I decided, was my first real kiss. I'd kissed Aria and Chris previously, and I hadn't liked either of them. *This* was what I'd been waiting for. *This* was the guy I wanted.

Yes.

My first kiss was with Adam Allegro, under the awning of an antique shop, soaking wet, with the rain cascading down around us. I wanted to stay in that bubble for the rest of forever.

Thirty-four

We ended up on the porch, absolutely drenched but blissful. He kissed me again and finally, regretfully, I opened the front door before Dad came bowling out. My intuition proved correct; he was standing on the other side of the door, waiting.

'Hi, Dad.'

'Did you have a good time?'

I could feel my face flush red.

'Yeah.' I grinned shyly at Adam and then back at my father to find that he wasn't even interested in me.

'Treating my girl well?' he asked.

My girl? I'd never seen him so protective.

'Yeah, of course.'

Awkward silence and then Adam shuffled his feet and stepped off the top step. 'I should probably go. Bye, Sylvie. It was nice to meet you, Mr Rivers.'

The rain was like a waterfall battering the roof, sliding off and splashing on the asphalt.

'How are you getting home, son?'

Adam stopped.

'Uh, walking.'

'I'll bring the car around. Can't have you getting hypothermia post-date with my daughter.'

My face broke into a smile. *Is this real?*

While we waited for the car to roll around I was overcome with joy, and threw my arms around Adam, smacking his cheek with a kiss. He laughed.

'Sylvie! Your dad might see!'

'I don't care! Thank you for tonight. It was awesome.'

'It was my pleasure.'

I sat in the back seat gazing at the back of Adam's head and wondering how long this would last. I wanted this guy for the rest of my life. I was quiet for the entire ride, while my dad and Adam chatted about school, exams, work and Christmas holidays. He was a hit. I knew he would be, but I hadn't expected Dave to give him a chance. We pulled up to his house. It looked so warm and cosy with the lights on in the living room. There was a woman at the window, sweeping back the curtain to peer out. She waved and Adam waved back.

'That's my mum,' he said, climbing out.

I climbed out too, to sit in the front.

'Thanks so much for the ride, Mr Rivers.'

'It's Dave,' my dad said. 'And you're welcome.'

'I'll text you,' he said to me.

'Okay.'

I was grinning from ear to ear and fighting every fibre of my being to let him go. He bent quickly and kissed me on the cheek, then took off up the driveway. Blushing, I climbed into the front seat and watched him disappear into the house. As we pulled away from the curb, he appeared in the window of his house and waved at us. I waved back, trying not to squeal with delight and alarm my father.

'He seems all right,' said Dad.

I texted Belle of the Books.

> Me: He KISSED me !! ON THE LIPS!

> Belle: Ooooooh! He LIKES you!

I smiled, picked a song on my phone and plugged it into the car radio.

'Now the clouds have gone and all the rain …' it began. Andrew's song.

'Clearly you are lovestruck and delusional,' my father remarked, 'because the rain is still pissing down.'

I laughed.

'Do you know this song? It's by a band called Reckless Abandon.'

'I know it. It was big long before you were born.'

'Belle's stepdad is in Reckless Abandon!'

'Well, how about that. Are they still around?'

'Yup.'

The rain was easing and he switched the windscreen wipers to a lower speed.

'Yeah well, I'm glad you've got Belle and Valerie,' he said gruffly.

'Yeah, they're cool.'

'Your mother's going to be away for the rest of the week.'

'She can stay away for the rest of my life if she wants.' I could taste the bitterness on my tongue.

'You don't mean that Sylvia.'

But I did.

Once home, I peeled off my dripping clothes and stepped into the warm shower. The mist engulfed me and I sang to an imaginary audience about bright sunshiney days. Cosy in my PJs, I caught sight of myself in the mirror. Brown, bobbed hair, tousled and damp. Face infused with a rosy hue. I looked so happy. My phone beeped.

Adam: Sleep well ☺

And again. My father this time – from down the hall.

Dave: Thought you should know the forecast for tomorrow is sunshine.

I laughed, climbed into bed and fell quickly into a deep sleep. Nothing could ruin this. Nothing!

Thirty-five

The sunshine stretched through the rest of the week. It was New Year's Eve. I was meeting Adam after his shift. The plan was to actually see the movie this time. I'd dressed in jeans, a checked shirt and sneakers, and revelled in the feeling of getting *me* back. I caught the bus into town, met Belle for lunch at the library café and talked non-stop about Adam and how much I liked him.

'But I'm freaking out,' I lamented. 'What if he finds out about the Chris incident? Or hears about Amelia Anderson and figures out it's me?'

'Sylvie, he won't. It sounds like he's really into you! Just go with it and enjoy it.' She sipped her milkshake. 'If the Chris 'thing' ever comes up, then cross that bridge when you come to it. Anyway, it seems like it's all old news.'

'Yeah, I guess,' I said. 'Ohhh, Belle, I like him so much!'

Belle laughed and clapped her hands.

'So are you going to try out the old you on Cate any time soon? See how she takes it?'

'Yeah. I think I will. But now I've got to run and meet Adam.'

We stood and hugged. I had so much love for that girl.

'Thank you so much for being here, Belle,' I said.

She giggled. 'That's what friends are for, dummy.'

Adam and I went to the movie and held hands the entire time which made retrieving handfuls of pop-corn a challenge, but one I was willing to take on. Afterwards we strolled through the streets and browsed the shops, procrastinating in all plausible ways about having to say goodbye. When finally we got to the bus stop he did that movie thing and stared into my eyes. I felt like I was on fire.

'You're beautiful, Sylvie.'

I nearly died.

Then with a kiss he jumped on the bus and sat waving at me like a little kid as it pulled away. I was overflowing with this ridiculous happiness that I never thought I would ever feel. Should I admit that I skipped a little as I headed in the direction of home?

'Sylvie the Slut!'

My blood went cold. A chill ran straight through

me and my pace quickened. Was I imagining that?

No.

'Turn around, bitch!'

It was a male voice. My palms were sweaty, heart in my throat. I wished I hadn't taken the empty side street. Footsteps behind me.

A hand roughly grabbed the back of my shirt and swung me around. Chris. He glared down at me with eyes full of fury.

'Think you'd get away with that prank, did ya?'

He spat on the ground next to my feet. I struggled to get out of his grasp. His grip tightened on my arm. I winced.

'I don't know what you're talking about,' I said, feigning confidence and failing, then crying out when his fist grazed my cheekbone. 'You think I wouldn't figure it out?' He hissed. 'Who the fuck else would Amelia Anderson be?'

'Fuck off, Chris.'

I tried to meet his eye. He slammed me back into a wall and I started to scream. He put his hand over my mouth and pushed his whole body against me. He smelt like alcohol. Tears leaked out of my eyes and my head and cheek throbbed.

'This feels familiar,' he leered.

'Oi! Get off her!' A man's voice barked to my left.

Chris jumped away from me as though I was electric and bolted in the other direction. Without having him to hold me up, I sank to the ground in a heap, trying to make myself as small as possible and cried the kind of tears that can't even find a sound. Footsteps shot past me in pursuit of him and gentle hands moved my own away from my face.

Crouching in front of me was a young woman with long dark hair. She had an art portfolio tucked under her arm and her face was filled with concern.

'What's your name?'

I tried to tell her, but all that came out of my mouth were sobs. She smoothed my hair and rubbed my shoulder.

'My name's Laura,' she told me. 'You're going to be okay. Do you think you can stand?'

A man appeared beside me, panting.

'The bastard jumped on a bus!' He said. He looked me over. 'We need to get you some help.'

Together the two of them helped me up and the man picked up my bag and handed it to Laura, who juggled it with her art portfolio and tried to support me with her other arm. My head throbbed and I could feel my face swelling up. My legs had turned to water from shock. It felt like Laura and the guy were all but dragging me between them. And the tears: they wet my face and hurt my throat. But still no volume.

I put a hand gingerly up to my cheek. It felt wet. I touched my fingers to my lips. Immediately I recognised the sharp, slick, metallic tang of blood. Until then I was the only one who'd ever drawn my own blood. And now he'd beaten me at my own game.

Did he have to take all of my power away?

They were helping me up some steps and talking to each other worriedly. *Or are they talking to me?* I'd retreated somewhere inside myself and only wanted to be alone with my pain. I didn't even care when they walked me over to a counter and pressed the shrill bell for service. It was ringing in my ears still when a police officer appeared, took one look at me and led us to a room with a table and chairs. He pulled out a chair and my two rescuers eased me into it, then sat down on either side of me. Laura took my hand. I wanted to tell her that I noticed, that I appreciated it, but all I could do was look at the floor.

My vision was blurred and the cop disappeared, then entered again with an icepack in a tea towel, which he offered to me. I felt like I couldn't even lift my arms. Laura took it from him, smoothed back my hair and held it to my cheek, just under my eye. I winced but remained silent.

'I'm Constable Josh Hurley,' the cop said. 'I don't mind if you call me Josh. What's your name?'

Honest to God I tried to answer him. I really did.

Sylvie the Second, my mind screamed. *Sylvie the Second. Sylvie the Slut.* But I had still not found my voice.

'If you can't tell me, I'm going to have to check your bag for identification. Do you consent to that?'

I managed to nod, but my synapses screamed out in pain. He reached for the bag and rummaged until he found my wallet. He pulled out my student ID.

'Sylvia Rivers?'

I nodded my head again, this time trying for less movement. He pushed my bag back towards me and picked up his pen, poised over a notepad.

'Sylvia, are you able to tell me what happened?'

Thirty-six

'You'll be fine,' the nurse said after she'd shone a torch in my eyes and assessed my aching face.

Her name badge told me that her name was Josie. She smiled sympathetically at me. Laura and her boyfriend, whose name I'd learnt was Max had stayed with me throughout the police ordeal and only left when Belle showed up with Valerie. Yup, when asked who I wanted to call, I'd elected not to inform the parents. Pamela Panic would get into a flap, and I kind of liked my dad the way he currently was. I knew he'd turn back into Damn-it-all Dave if he found out what happened.

Belle had her arm around me and her head on my shoulder. Valerie sat carefully listening to the nurse's instructions.

'Take her to ED if there's any change in her vision,

if she starts vomiting, or slurring her speech …'

Meanwhile I sat stiffly, only vaguely aware of what was going on, not registering the weight of Belle's head on my shoulder, the comfort of her arm around me.

'Have the STI checks been done?' Josie the nurse was asking me. I nodded, mute. I'd used up all of my voice giving the statement at the police station.

Belle cleared her throat.

'He gave her chlamydia but she's been treated for it.'

Valerie shook her head and held onto my hand.

'Okay,' Josie said as I stared ahead at nothing. 'Poor girl. Take two Panadol tablets every four to six hours for any pain and don't hesitate to call if you have any concerns. Look after yourself, Sylvie. See you later.'

Valerie and Belle led me out the door and settled me into the car.

'I'm going to have to take you home, sweetheart,' Valerie said. 'Your dad needs to know what's happening. I'm happy to talk for you as much as I can though, okay?'

I nodded mutely and winced again. I couldn't comprehend the mess I'd got myself into.

The moment the cop had asked me what had happened, my mouth opened and all the bottled up hatred I felt towards Chris – all the vitriol, the venom – had been unleashed. Laura had squeezed my hand the whole time. The cop wrote down everything I said, took down my contact details and said someone would be in touch. He spoke to Valerie on the phone and told her to meet me next door at the medical centre. I had a headache and bruising on my jaw and cheekbone. When I considered what Chris might have done if my two saviours hadn't chased him away, I felt as though I'd waded out into a too-cold sea. I shivered despite the heat and kept my face down, so Belle and Valerie couldn't see my tears. I felt so hurt and humiliated.

Most of all I felt afraid.

What was I afraid of? Well, everything.

What if they made me press charges? Would I have to go to court? How would my parents react? How would everyone else react?

Adam?

As if reading my mind, Belle asked, 'Did you text Adam?'

I couldn't suppress the groan that escaped me.

'No. How can I? He doesn't know about the Chris thing in the first place so how do I explain this?' I sighed, despairingly.

'Sylvie. He knows about Chris.'

The seabed underneath me dropped away. And then I realised that I wasn't surprised.

Belle took a breath and when she exhaled she put her head back against the seat and closed her eyes. She looked tired and drained and I realised then – the way it suddenly dawns on you that it's pouring with rain and your clothes are on the line and you wonder how you didn't notice earlier – that Belle was carrying a lot of my burdens. And she was sinking under the weight. I needed to sort myself out. Why had it taken me so long to do anything?

Thank God for Valerie. Belle and I sat outside, side by side, while Valerie explained everything she knew to Damn-it-all Dave. Belle and I didn't speak while we waited. I had no idea how to articulate how sorry I was for giving her all of my troubles and expecting her to hold me up. Part of me wanted her to impart some of her wise words as she usually did, but it seemed she had no vocabulary for this situation. I hoped she might come up with a quote from one of her books, but she was quiet. She was a dried-up well of worn-out wisdom. She'd given me so much and I hadn't listened. I wondered why she didn't hate me.

My nerves gave a sharp jolt as I heard footsteps behind us.

'Sylvie?' Valerie's voice was gentle. 'Your dad wants to see you, honey.'

That old anxiety was at it again – hosting a full-on drum and bass rave. I hoped its lease would end soon. I looked at Belle, at her huge beautiful eyes and tangle of hair. She gave me a crooked smile of encouragement. How did she find that kind of strength inside her? I hugged her tightly and breathed in her lavender shampoo.

'I'm sorry, Belle,' I whispered.

'You have nothing to be sorry for,' she said and let me go.

Valerie threw her arms around me and gave me a kiss on the cheek.

'None of this is your fault, Sylvie,' she told me. 'We're all going to help you get through it.'

She was so motherly and comforting and suddenly I became aware of how much I missed my own mother, and those runaway tears escaped again. Valerie wiped them away and smoothed my hair.

'Your parents love you a lot. Sometimes people just don't show it very well.'

They got in the car and waited until I had gone inside. I could hear the engine start as I walked numbly towards the living room. My father was standing up, leaning on the back of the chair with his eyes closed. They opened when he heard my footfall and he straightened up. For what felt like ages, but was probably only a few seconds, we stood staring at each other. Unsaid words and roughly concealed emotions suspended between us, electric, sparking, snapping.

'Oh, Sylvie!' My father was crying (I'm serious, he actually cried), and the spell was broken.

'Daddy!' I sobbed, rushing into his open arms. He was so strong and smelt so familiar, of fresh moss and cool earth, a hint of coffee. All of a sudden I was his little girl again, and he was comforting me when I fell off the swing and hit the ground with a jarring thud. But then he tensed and his grip on me slackened slightly. His eyes, wet from tears, were fixed on something behind me. My first thought was Chris.

He'd found me. He was going to kill me. Fear surged. I clutched Dad's arm.

'Sylvie?'

And there it was. A voice I had heard almost daily since the minute I was born. A voice that sang me lullabies and coached me through making my first ever lasagne, that rose to a shrill pitch when its owner was angry or alarmed, that told me once upon a time that it loved me.

I turned, and there stood my mother, on the threshold of the living room looking at the scene before her, wonder mingling with hurt. Her face crumpled when she saw the mess on mine, and she dropped her bag at her feet. Tentatively, she held out her arms, and just as tentatively, I walked across the space between my two parents and let her wrap them around me.

'I'm so sorry, my baby,' she whispered and I breathed in her perfume.

She was so warm. I was home.

Thirty-seven

We spent some time together as a family, discussing what our next move should be. I had to explain the entire sordid story to both of them, during which my mum cried and blew her nose and my dad sat numbly staring at the coffee table, jaw clenching and unclenching. Eventually, Mum left to return to her friend's house where she said would continue to stay.

· 'But you're welcome to come and visit any time you like, darling,' she assured me. 'I'll see you tomorrow. We'll have coffee.'

'Why can't you come home?' I said.

She shook her head sadly. 'Your dad and I need some time apart, Sylvie.'

'Are you getting divorced?' my voice trembled.

They glanced awkwardly at each other.

'Let's just focus on you for now, love,' said my dad.

'*No!*' My voice was stronger than any of us expected. 'This isn't just about me. If you want to help me then we need to get some family counselling or something,' I said. I looked at the two of them, feeling some authority. 'How can you help me if you can't even help yourselves?'

My mum cleared her throat. 'All right, honey, we'll look into it tomorrow.' She gave me a kiss and started down the driveway.

'Mum!'

She turned back to face me, twisting her dark blonde hair around her finger.

'How's Cate?'

A melancholy smile.

'She misses you.'

My mother came over for coffee the following day. She wanted to go out but I didn't feel up to it. She'd brought with her a list of counsellors she'd found in the Yellow Pages.

'Would you like to choose one?'

I settled on a lady called Claire Davidson, and my dad called her immediately and made an appointment.

'We'll see her in a week,' he told us.

I fished out the card Alannah had given me and handed it to him.

'I want to go here too. Just me.'

He took the card from me and inspected it before

handing it to my mum.

'It's free. The Family Planning doctor did a referral, but when they rang me I didn't answer the phone.' I looked at my feet. 'I think it would be good for me.'

My parents looked at each other and then back at me.

'We think so too, sweetheart,' said Mum.

After Mum had left I asked Dad if he could leave the house for a while.

'I need to see Adam,' I explained. 'But I don't want to leave the house and I don't want you here. No offence.'

He smiled wearily.

'None taken. I'm happy to go out for a while but you let me know if you need me and I'll come straight back.'

I nodded. 'Okay, Dad. Thanks.'

I was pacing in my room wringing my hands, anxiety body-slamming the walls of my ribcage when he rang the doorbell.

Now I was walking towards the door, feeling the magnetic pull of Adam's anxiety as I got closer. I wondered if he could feel mine. Hand on the door handle, I took a deep breath and opened it.

His mouth dropped open when he saw me, and the next thing I knew he'd pulled me into a fierce embrace.

'I'll kill them!' He vowed, planting kisses all over my face and touching all my bruises.

I led him to my bedroom and we sat down as one on the bed.

Out with it.

'It was Chris ...'

Adam's rage propelled him back to standing position and he paced back and forth just as I had been doing minutes before, spitting out a vast array of expletives and then: 'Why?!'

Flooded with shame I began to tell him what had happened all that time ago at the party.

'I know all this!' he interrupted, and then checked himself. 'Sorry,' he said, calmer. 'I know he ... I know what he did to you.'

WTF! 'How?'

He shoved his hands in his pockets and shifted his weight.

'News travels. And Chris likes to brag. What I want to know is why did he do *this* (here he freed his hands and gesticulated wildly towards my face) to you?'

So I told him about my revenge via Facebook and how Chris had figured out it was me. I watched his face carefully for his reaction. He sat back down and stared at me like he'd never seen me before ... And then burst out laughing.

'Sylvie Rivers! What a dark horse!' he sputtered and then kissed me. 'I didn't know you had it in you.'

I was beyond confused.

'So ... you're not angry at me?'

He stopped laughing and looked at me seriously.

'No.'

'You're not … disgusted by me?'

'No. Why would I be?'

'Ugh!' I exclaimed, standing up and burying my face in my hands. 'Because he gave me the clap! Because I was raped! Because I'm dirty and disgusting and – '

'Stop it, Sylvie. He gave you chlamydia when he *raped* you. You didn't ask for it. You didn't have any control of it! And you are not dirty or disgusting.' He grabbed my arm as I paced past him, turned it over and kissed my palm.

I was too caught up in my head; off guard, and so I didn't have time to react when his thumb moved on my wrist, displaying the cuts that my sleeves had faithfully kept secret.

No blood. No breath. No feeling except one: horror.

I stared at the top of his head as he took in the two red lines, carefully knitted back together. He exhaled heavily and I could feel it tickling my skin. He let go of my wrist.

'God, Sylvie. I don't know if I'm ready for all this.'

Exactly what I thought you'd say. 'I don't expect you to have to deal with it.'

He looked at me with something like a question on his face.

'What?'

I sat opposite him.

'I don't expect you to want to stick around. That's

why I hadn't told you anything. Because I was scared.' My voice wasn't working as well as I wanted it to. 'I'm getting counselling. Because I want to help myself. It's not fair of me to expect you to carry me.'

Adam was shaking his head at me, as if not comprehending.

'Sylvie, *what?!*'

I was snuffling in a super ugly way, attempting to regain composure but feeling so worn down I couldn't do it. He ran his hands through his thick dark hair in that way he did, and sighed heavily. I could almost see the weight of what I'd just handed him making his shoulders sag. He took my hand and I wiped my nose with the back of my other one, not caring anymore if I was being unattractive.

'I didn't say I was breaking up with you.'

I did a classic movie moment double take. *Huh?*

On his face was the gravest expression in the history of expressions.

'I totally agree that you need some counselling. You've had a rough time and you've been treated like shit and you don't deserve it. If you promise to go to all of your counselling sessions and try your best to work through all this then I will stick around. The Sylvie I like is smart and funny and awkward and weird and *happy*. I like her smile.'

I grinned like the Cheshire Cat. 'You think I'm awkward?'

He laughed, reached out and picked something up.

It was the wire crown. He looked at it for a moment, and then lifted the crown up and placed it carefully on my head. 'My favourite thing about you. Is there anything you need me to do, my queen?'

I snuggled into his side, content at that moment for him to do nothing but hold me. And then I thought of something.

'Actually, I'd like you to come to the hospital with me. There's someone I want you to meet.'

Thirty-eight

We waited three weeks. I wanted to make sure my bruises had gone completely, no trace left behind. By that time we had been to family therapy with Claire twice and I'd been to my youth counsellor, Awhina, once. She had begun by getting me involved in a support group for young people who have a sibling with mental illness. I hadn't been to a meeting yet – the next one was two days away – and I was nervous but also hopeful. There were others like me. I wanted to know how they coped; what they did to keep themselves 'safe,' to use the counselling terminology.

I'd also heard from the police. They were pressing charges against Chris, and were in the process of taking statements from his circle of friends. I was afraid they would up the ante with their bullying, but I guess they'd been warned against it. They weren't stupid, after all. I would have to appear in court at some point, which was terrifying, and Chris would not be returning to school.

We'd spent the previous Saturday at Adam's, whose parents had hosted a barbeque for friends and family. I was introduced to his mum and dad, siblings and nephews who welcomed me as though I was one of them. I brought Belle along, who kept blushing furiously whenever Adam's cousin Evan walked past.

My parents had officially decided to separate and my mum found a small flat to rent while they sorted out all that stuff that grown-ups have to sort out when they split up. I felt like the family therapy sessions had shed some light on the hidden issues that my parents kept skirting around, and I knew we probably wouldn't go to many more, although I would continue to see my youth counsellor for as long as it took.

I wasn't as angry at my parents anymore since both counsellors had encouraged me to see things from their point of view. Cate's mental health problems weren't only scary for me. While I was worried that I was going to catch her disorder, my parents were worried that they were responsible for giving it to her. While I was terrified that I was going to lose my sister, my parents were frightened of losing their daughter. While I felt somehow blamed for Cate's situation, I learned that actually my parents had turned a lot of their blame inwards, and what was directed at me was just seeping through the cracks of the load they were carrying inside themselves.

None of us were feeling strong and that manifested as anger, in what was already a fractious environment. We were all making an effort to change that.

I hadn't touched alcohol since Christmas and didn't miss it at all. I didn't feel like I had any need for it with all these new supports around me. Alcohol, I realised, never listened to me anyway. It didn't make me feel better, it just numbed me to the point where all I was capable of feeling was nausea.

My cuts were healing well. I'm not going to lie, sometimes it was still the first thing that sprang to mind when the going got tough. But cuts couldn't speak for me, and I was learning better ways of managing and communicating with the people around me. I held out hope that the scars would fade, and I'd be able to wear short sleeves again in summer.

When Adam and I walked into the ward to see Cate, I almost turned and bolted. If he hadn't had my hand clasped reassuringly in his I probably would have. I hadn't seen her since that horrible Christmas Day and butterflies were fluttering chaotically in my tummy. How would she react this time? I took some deep breaths and looked at Adam.

'We'll be fine,' he said. 'Your parents say she's getting better.'

'I know,' I breathed. 'But you should've seen her last time, Adam! It was –'

'Sylvie!'

I broke off and stared at the girl standing at the other end of the hallway. My big sister, clear-eyed and alert, smiling widely at us in welcome. And then we were skipping towards each other until we collided in the middle, and grabbed on, never wanting to let go.

'I've missed you so much!' we said in unison, and laughed.

'I'm so sorry I scared you at Christmas,' Cate cried. 'You look like you again! I like your hair.'

'I decided to cut it after seeing you'd cut yours.'

Cate grimaced. 'Yeah. I talked a student nurse into giving me scissors.'

We laughed again and she grabbed my hand.

'Are you going to introduce me to your friend?'

'Oh! Catie, this is Adam. *My boyfriend.*'

Adam stuck his hand out and Cate took it, smiling.

'Nice to meet you Adam, Sylvie's boyfriend.'

'Nice to meet you too, Cate, Sylvie's sister.'

'I hope she told you some good things about me.'

'She never told me anything bad.'

Cate sat with her arm linked through mine and listened intently to stories Adam and I told her. She was so out of touch with the world outside the building. Adam and I talked about exams and New Year's and how we met ('she eats too much pizza'), deliberately avoiding the soap opera that had been my life until recently. She would find out soon enough. We'd brought Cate some white chocolate – her favourite. She ripped it open and devoured it.

'Do you know what I've missed more than anything while I've been here?' she grinned wickedly at Adam.

He smiled at her. 'What?'

'Pizza!'

Within minutes Adam was on his phone calling work. 'It's being delivered and is on the house,' he said, hanging up.

'Oh, Sylvie, you have to keep him!' Cate exclaimed, jumping up and down in her seat and clapping her hands like a little girl.

'Yeah, I like him a lot.'

After we'd demolished the pizzas, we said our good-byes. Cate gave me a kiss on the cheek and whispered, 'I'll see you on Friday.'

I was confused.

'Do you want me to come in on Friday?'

She started laughing.

'No! I'm coming home for weekend leave. If it goes well I might be able to be discharged. I was trying to keep it a secret but I'm so excited!'

'Ohmigod! I've got the latest season of *Modern Family*! We can make popcorn and binge-watch.'

We held hands all the way to the door where she gave me one last hug and whispered, 'I like him.'

I was so happy. I gave her a mischeivous grin, one that I'd learned from her.

'Back off, sis, he's mine!'

Cate's eyes crinkled, she threw her head back and laughed that joyous, lively, wild laugh that I hadn't heard for so long. As the doors closed, we blew each other a kiss. Out on the street, I grabbed Adam's hand and smacked a kiss on his jaw.

'Okay. What was that for?'

'You know!' I said. 'For being you.'

At home, there was a letter waiting for me:

> Dear Sylvie,
>
> I wanted to thank you for having the courage to go to the police about what Chris did to you. It took a lot of courage and I'm sorry it happened to you. He did the same thing to me. At the time I thought it was because he liked me so much, but now I know he didn't like me at all. If he did, he never would've done what he did. I've gone to the police and told them my story in support of yours, and I'm glad they're pressing charges. I never would've done this if it wasn't for you.
>
> Thank you.

It wasn't signed.

Epilogue

Adam and I were at Belle's. It was a hot day and we were packing a chilly bin full of ice cream and fizzy drinks. We were going to a festival that marked the end of the tour for Andrew. Valerie was driving us and would then leave us while she hung out with the band. She reckoned Andrew would let us go backstage.

Adam kept checking his phone – I assumed to check the time – until the doorbell rang. Belle stopped packing and looked up frowning. Valerie's footsteps padded down the hall towards the door.

'Wonder who that is?' Belle said.

Adam shuffled his feet and put his phone back in his pocket. 'Uh, I invited Evan.'

It was like someone had spilt red food colouring under Belle's skin. The stain spread quickly, filling her face.

'Adam!' She hissed. 'I can't see him! Look at my hair!'

I laughed as Valerie ushered Evan into the kitchen. He looked almost as awkward as Belle did.

'Hi guys. Nice place, Belle …'

Belle busied herself repacking the already packed chilly bin. 'Thanks,' she squeaked. I wondered if her internal dialogue was as rough on her as mine was.

We piled into the sweltering car and set off on the road, climbing out again when we reached the venue, a farm. Our skin was slick with sweat and we fanned our faces with our hands and squinted into the sun. We scouted the grass for a good spot, Adam and I walking ahead slightly to let some conversation take place between Belle and Evan, and found a good space next to a grassy knoll where we laid out our picnic blanket.

There were trailers selling kebabs, dumplings, chips and hot dogs, and while the boys went to get us some food, Belle and I talked about Evan.

'Do you think he likes me?'

'Definitely!'

We ate, we laughed, we sang, we danced. The sun was hot in the sky; sunblock was compulsively re-applied; ice cream melted and ran down our hands. I was overheating because I didn't want to show the scars on my arm. There are some consequences you have to live with.

Among the throngs of summery festival-goers I

noticed Lorelei. She was wearing a flower crown and a sundress and, to my relief, was with two girls I'd never seen before. She was laughing as she caught my eye. We nodded to each other in acknowledgement and exchanged the ghost of a smile before one of her friends linked arms with her and pulled her away. That chapter was closed.

Somewhere in the middle of Andrew's set I heard him say my name. My head whipped to my left, where Belle was watching me with a look of effervescent excitement.

'Did he just say this song goes out to Sylvie?' I asked her.

She grabbed my hand and pulled me up.

'Yes!' She yelled, and the first notes of a familiar song blared out of the speakers.

I smiled so hard I thought my face might crack. Adam's hand was warm in mine and I started dancing next to Belle, twirling under Adam's arm. It was all good. Really good. But not all chapters were closed. I still had to face the repercussions of Chris and the court case. I still had to deal with separated parents and a sick sister who was better for now, but maybe not forever.

There were bridges I would have to cross when I came to them. There were bridges I would have to build and ones I had burned that I would have to mend. I was learning that life is really about which bridge you choose, where it leads, the unexpected rickety bits in the middle and how you navigate it. If you fell, hopefully you'd have some people to lift you up until you could put your feet on the ground.

I had learned that I had those people, and some of them were dancing in the sun next to me, laughing and singing at the top of their lungs.

This song was for me. I could see that now. All the people there could see it too. And me. They could see me.

Now the clouds have gone and all the rain:
it's a sky-blue kind of day.
All those things that make it hard to see.
Now it's nothing but sunshine –
bright, bright sunshine – for you and me …

I am Sylvie Rivers. Not second. Not invisible.

If you need help, speak up.

Youthline: www.youthline.co.nz

What's Up: www.whatsup.co.nz

The Lowdown: www.thelowdown.info

Rainbow Youth: www.ry.org.nz

Headspace: www.headspace.org.nz

Or talk to your school guidance counsellor or an adult you can trust.